Praise for
The American Quarter

"Douaihy's writing is of extreme beauty, concise but full of life… with the fate of its characters intersecting and intertwining… 'Transforming the mediocrity of everyday life' says Douaihy, 'is the miracle that writing can accomplish.' When it comes to *The American Quarter*, the miracle truly occurs…"
—Eglal Errera, *Le Monde des livres*

"A novel the power of which many documentarians would envy…"
—William Irigoyen, *La Cité*

"The work of a remarkable writer…imbued with intelligence and humanity…deep empathy with those he writes about…Not only does Douaihy love his city, but…its people…His heroes, ordinary people, struggle in the middle of a story that extends beyond them, in search of a sense of dignity…"
—Sonia Dayan-Herzbrun, *En attendant Nadeau*

"Douaihy's work should reach, and charm, wide…audiences."
—Marcia Lynx Qualey, *Qantara*

The American Quarter

by Jabbour Douaihy

translated by Paula Haydar

Interlink Books

An imprint of Interlink Publishing Group, Inc.
Northampton, Massachusetts

First published in 2018 by

Interlink Books
An imprint of Interlink Publishing Group, Inc.
46 Crosby Street, Northampton, Massachusetts 01060
www.interlinkbooks.com

Library of Congress Cataloging-in-Publication Data
Names: Duwayhåi, Jabbåur author. | Haydar, Paula, 1965- translator.
Title: The American quarter / Jabbour Douaihy ; translated by Paula Haydar.
Other titles: òHayy al-Amåirkåan. English
Description: Northampton, MA : Interlink Books, 2017.
Identifiers: LCCN 2017031323 | ISBN 9781566560306
Classification: LCC PJ7820.U92 H3913 2017 | DDC 892.7/37--dc23
LC record available at https://lccn.loc.gov/2017031323

Cover image:
Arabesque Hanging Glass Beads © Eliane Haykal | Dreamstime

Excerpts from the Quran are from a translation by A. J. Arberry
[http://www.theonlyquran.com/quran/Al-i'Imran/English_Arthur_John_Arberry]
p. 17: Surat Aal Imran, Verse 53; Surat Aal Imran, Verse 54; Surat Aal Imran, Verse 55.
p. 115: Surat al-Baraqa, Verse 216
p. 121: Surat al-Baraqa, Verse 216; Surat aal-Tawba, Verse 41
p. 135: Surat al-An'aan, Verse 45
p. 136: Surat Aal Imran, Verse 176
p. 138: Surat Aal Imran, Verse 167

Excerpt on page 115 from the poem, "I pass by your name," by Mahmoud Darwish.

Printed and bound in the United States of America

To request our complete 48-page catalog, please call us
toll free at 1-800-238-LINK, visit our website at
www.interlinkbooks.com, or write to
Interlink Publishing, 46 Crosby Street, Northampton, MA 01060

1

After a fruitless search for something to put on between his feet and the cold floor, Abdelrahman Bakri emerged barefooted from his bedroom and hurried toward the bathroom. With age, it had become more and more pressing that he take care of his morning needs as quickly as possible. But all of a sudden, and in accordance with a daily habit that had begun to take hold of him the day he'd brought home the big color television—a habit his wife thought only death *might* stop him from doing—Abdelrahman stopped short in the middle of the space between his bedroom door and the bathroom located beneath the stairway leading to the top floor. With his right hand grasping at the crotch of his striped pajamas, an indication of the urgency of his situation, he stood there scanning his surroundings in search of the remote control.

Now this Abdelrahman of ours, who they called *al-Mashnouq*, or "the Hanged Man"—a family nickname whose origins were long forgotten—resides in the American Quarter, so named for its association with the now abandoned Evangelical School, in whose crumbling buildings a branch of the dreaded

Syrian Intelligence Agency had been headquartered for many years. The quarter overlooks the city's river, making it impossible for residents to get to their homes without climbing the endless stairways that had drawn wrinkles on the neighborhood, and resembled the rivulets that melting snows had etched upon the surface of the mountains. Everyone would help out whenever anyone needed to transport furniture or carry the sick, and those who could afford it would solicit the services of porters from the nearby vegetable market. Al-Mashnouq lived with his wife, who was older than him, and their five children, in a sandstone house that a middle-class family of wheat traders had abandoned a half-century earlier when their sons settled down in an affluent neighborhood west of the city. Here and there one could still see remnants of the building's original embellishments—a rose-shaped carving on the marble mantel above the heavy door of resinous wood, or the crumbling stone etchings along the edge of the roof—all manifestations of its current wretched state that betrayed the presence of a former life in the American Quarter. That was before Tripoli was inundated by the poor folk from the nearby mountains who could no longer subsist on harvesting the locally grown *Imm Husein* apricots, or any other fruit trees for that matter. Out of necessity, al-Mashnouq had had to make do with the two rooms on the ground floor of the building, plus the space that everything under the sun passed through during the day, in the middle of which was the staircase leading to the two upstairs rooms and from where the intermittent shouting between him and his co-renter and housemate, Bilal Muhsin, got blurted, directly in his family members' faces.

Al-Mashnouq had found the used 24-inch Philips television on someone's table at a Friday flea market. He asked the seller to package it up as best he could in an empty cardboard box, which the seller did, also tossing in some balls of white Styrofoam packing material, along with an owner's manual for a gas stove, written in Chinese.

"Here you go, just like new," he joked.

Al-Mashnouq strained to pick it up and tried to lug it under his arm, but was forced after nearly dislocating his shoulder to carry it with two hands. He lifted the box to nose level, which made walking very difficult. Several times he paused, panting, as he ascended the stairs. There in front of everyone he tore the tape off the box and brandished the remote control as if it were a bit of war booty. Then he busied himself designing a proper location for it, straightening the TV just right after circling around it, or turning it in various directions, after which he would move the sofa to position it in accordance with the new location. Finally, he decided the best spot was on the third step of the staircase, though he hoped none of Bilal Muhsin's children would knock it over in their rush down the stairs. Next, he donated the old black-and-white television to the neighborhood kids, who immediately began taking it apart to see what mysterious contents were hiding behind its screen. They poked and prodded the various tubes and wires from every angle. And he arranged with the Muhsin family to pay him a monthly fee for the cable stations, in return for which they could come downstairs and sit and watch the programs there in the entryway any time they pleased. Al-Mashnouq maintained exclusive control of the remote, carried it with him at all times, and would forget it on purpose in his jacket pocket when he went out to the market. He eventually decided to attach it to the big key that opened the massive front door, whose locks he refused to replace because he didn't want to have too many keys around the house.

Maybe as a result of the excessive force he used when pressing the buttons on the remote control, or due to some sort of defect in the used television set, from time to time the TV volume would blast out at maximum level the moment it was turned on. Or, out of the blue, the volume would suddenly increase to the maximum setting without anyone touching it. And that is precisely what happened this particular morning when al-Mashnouq, failing to use his time wisely for the purpose of urinating, and opting instead before that to press the green button on the remote control, set loose a cacophony of blaring noises from the television set. It was a mishmash of screaming voices in a foreign language, an incessant whistling sound, the chiming of a bell, and loud applause.

This is how, in the wee hours before sunrise on this particular morning, al-Mashnouq managed to wake up everyone in his household and all the neighbors, too, to the blaring sound of a women's freestyle wrestling match taking place inside a pool of brightly colored mud, before an audience of overexcited men who were shouting and smoking, which was airing on one of the American sports channels. The blast of sound came as a loud shock to al-Mashnouq as well. He was bewildered trying to decide whether to fiddle with the remote and find the volume control button or to heed the urgent call of nature that he could no longer resist. The situation lasted a few seconds, just long enough to bring his terrified wife out of her bedroom to ask who had died. She saw him standing there, the events having forced him to adjust the volume with some difficulty, and went back to her room, mumbling to God, "Give us strength in our final days." Meanwhile, the children responded loudly from their room with sharp complaints, despite having grown accustomed, along with everyone else in the American Quarter, to the dawn call to prayer that emanated from the nearby Attar Mosque. It usually made them turn in their beds when it sounded, or set them muttering words in their rattled sleep until it ended.

Intisar, Bilal Muhsin's wife who was asleep in her room upstairs, was also awakened by the sound blast from the television. Her heart pounded like a big drum. In an involuntary movement, she pushed away her spoiled little daughter who clung to her as if to a tree and wouldn't go to sleep unless her head was nestled on her mother's bosom. At dawn she would resume giving her mother her fill of kicks and hugs once the two mattresses that had been pushed together provided her with an open playground in the absence of her father Bilal who often disappeared from home for days at a time, without warning or excuse. Intisar got up in stages. She sat up and braced her back against the damp wall. She took a deep breath and stretched her shoulders back as if she could use her body as a dam in the face of the day about to inundate her with an attack. She closed her eyes and searched between breaths for her sleeping daughter's hand between the blankets. She brought the little hand to her mouth, pressed her lips to it at length, and drew in a deep breath. She breathed in life force and oxygen from her daughter, in a never-ending kiss, and didn't slide her hand back under the warm blankets until her fear subsided and her heart gradually went back to its normal rhythm.

"God help us. What a way to start the day," she whispered to herself.

She slid one leg out from under the blankets, raised it up a little, and inspected her toenails in the dim morning light that had begun to creep in. The red polish was still there in little patches she let rub off on their own. She had painted them herself, though she wasn't accustomed to doing it. She'd locked herself inside the room and painted them. She heard that men like seeing polish on women's toenails, all men except Bilal Muhsin, as it turned out. Later she started doing it for herself, finding pleasure in tenderly applying a new color she'd bought after bathing and savoring the rare opportunity to be alone in the house with her own body.

The day heats up. The din of activity begins to ascend the stairways of the quarter. She glances over at the other bedroom where the boys are sleeping, in case her eldest son Ismail has taken her unawares at night and snuck back into his bed without waking her. Ismail, who had stolen her sleep and her heart by disappearing two weeks earlier, leaving no note, no explanation. She wakes the others, lifting off their blankets. She combs the girl's hair first, hurting her as she does. She gently slaps her daughter's thigh as she dresses her, reminding her not to dangle her skinny legs out of the opening at the back of the school bus that takes her to Al-Iman Charitable School, and swing them at passersby. She sits and dresses the youngest boy while instructing his older brother to bring him back home early and not take him along to the internet café where he spends all his time playing games and looking at dirty pictures, while his disabled little brother stands behind him watching and learning depraved behavior from him. She reminds him not to let anyone make fun of him in the streets and to watch out for him like Ismail had done.

She finishes getting dressed and files in with the children as they make their morning departure. They cross the al-Mashnouq 'checkpoint' where he sits, barricaded for eternity in his armchair. Hearing their commotion, he raises his fat belly as much as he can and casts his gaze in Intisar's direction as she tries her best to move along quietly in a straight line. The group stops in front of the television, and even if only for a few seconds, the little ones watch the scene unfolding on the screen. She always has to nudge them out the door. Al-Mashnouq quickly changes the channel the moment he hears their footsteps, switching to CNN or the Chasse et Pêche hunting and fishing channel, because he doesn't want them to discover what all of them already know—that he was watching women's wrestling or the endless parade of beauties marching up and down the runway on the Fashion Channel. The moment she makes it past him, Intisar can feel him ogling her again, especially whenever Bilal is out of the house. He steals long glances at her behind, whose shape can barely be discerned under her new, loose-fitting robe, as she slips through the front door and steps outside with her meager entourage.

They walk along, heading up the quarter's stairway like every morning, one stair at a time, right through the puddles of rain from the night before, paced by the young hobbled one with the weak leg who flees from the toil of walking with whatever little distractions he might find along the way. He stops to watch the coppersmith as he pounds the sheet of white copper he's been hammering since early morning with his special hammer, and so his little sister, overjoyed for finally acquiring a schoolbag with straps she can wear on her back, stops to watch too. Intisar follows them as they poke along, until they turn right at the top of the stairs, and she loses sight of them before they reach the main street whose cars can be heard honking their horns for some reason or other, or for no reason at all. There they will go their separate ways—the girl to school, the second oldest son to the car repair shop where he'll be consumed by grease and oil and he'll associate with thugs, and the third to the Children with Disabilities Center. Meanwhile, Intisar starts to make her way back down toward the river and the city during her daily patch of free time.

The sky has started to clear a little, though the precipitation from the storm still runs down the steps despite the blue sky, dragging with it all the litter from the higher neighborhoods and redistributing it equally into every corner of the American Quarter. Students in the primary grades ascend the stairs in groups, against the water flow, joyfully stomping their feet in the little muddy puddles and splashing water in their own faces and hitting their friends, too. Intisar's steps pound inside her head as she heaves her heavy body downhill, so she slows down beside the pile of discarded bones with flies buzzing around it outside the butcher shop and continues all the way down to the last wide step, her body heaving slightly to the left as if she were carrying a heavy stone over her heart.

She ultimately lands on the straight road that runs parallel to the river. Her body continues to resist her, so she walks toward the produce market. The owner of the bakery appears before her, standing outside his door hand-tossing a piece of dough. He directs his gaze into the distance, waiting for someone to arrive. He notices her and heads inside, to get away from her. To steer clear of her. She doesn't like his embroidered white skullcap, or his long shirt, or his plump round face. He eats four helpings before burrowing into his bed at night. He sleeps by himself, without a wife. People said they gave him electric shocks while he was in prison for many long years and it made him impotent. She follows after him and stands silently in the doorway, questioning him with her eyes. He knows what she wants. Starting the day after Ismail disappeared, she stands there in his face, every day, and they cast glances back and forth. When he can't stand it anymore, he turns around toward the oven, pretending to be busy with his work, and waves her off, saying, "Put your faith in the Lord of All Creation, Woman..."

She gives him a dirty look and nods her head in a gesture promising a punishment entirely out of her reach. She continues on her way to the vegetable market. The morning crowd calls out to her. If she were to faint there in that spot, as she fears she might today, the passersby and the cart vendors would rush to pick her up and sprinkle water on her face to bring her back to consciousness. People from all walks of life descend from the villages: unveiled Christian women, those tough ladies who drive a hard bargain; farmers smelling strongly of moist soil during the wet winter season who arrive at the city souks bright and early; men, teachers, workers, the most sophisticated types—all pour in one after the other from the new neighborhoods sprawling toward the sea. They come back to the souks on the premise of going shopping, but mostly they just like to entertain themselves by strolling around in those cramped neighborhoods where they were born. They saunter over to the Khan al-Saboun, the Soap Market, in order to carry back with them a familiar scent that reminds them of their childhood, and if by chance it comes time for the noon prayers, they go inside one of the little Mamluk mosques.

Intisar Muhsin plunges in among them. They propel her along the narrow passageway behind the wooden vendor tables and the pushcarts driven by poor foreigners peddling their winter vegetables. They come from afar, walking from countries that got fed up with them as well, for many long days, amid the dust of the treeless roads, with their heads exposed to the burning sun. They stop here to sell everything that will sell. The folks from the nearby neighborhoods complain that they're eating up other people's livelihoods and that they don't spend any money. They pile up on top of each other in tiny rooms, get up with the dawn prayers, conglomerate at the intersections and chase after cars, shout to passersby, and compete fiercely to secure work and drag their heavy loads like beasts of burden.

She takes to the narrow sidewalks to get away from all their commotion, and walks beside the high shop doors with the heavy iron doorknockers, and where the people zoom by in every direction on their little motor scooters. A car speeds past the pedestrians and splashes a big puddle of muddy rainwater onto them that had formed in the middle of the main street. Someone always curses the driver in a loud voice, and the driver in turn replies with an insulting hand gesture. She thought about getting a taxi to take her to the other side of the city, but she didn't want to get stuck between passengers pressing their bodies against her, intentionally or otherwise. She'd rather walk alone. Her legs were in good working order and her posture was firm and straight and drew men's eyes in her direction, even after having given birth to four children. She crosses over from a sidewalk blocked by a heap of household garbage to a pool of water, to the strong smell of boric acid emanating from the soap factory—the old man sitting outside its doorway doesn't notice her—to the smell of the stickleback fish coming from the basket of a foot peddler. Suddenly, the call to prayer blasts out from the purse hanging from her shoulder.

"Oh God. It's Ismail!"

She reaches into her purse for the phone, but cannot manage to find the opening. She has lost control of her own hand. The purse falls to the ground. The phone stops ringing and tears start streaming down her cheeks. Ismail had given her that phone and had written instructions for her on a piece of paper, at the top of which he wrote: *"Bismillah ar-rahman ar-rahim,"* In the name of God the merciful, the compassionate.

"And I am supposed to carry it around like this, in my hand?"

"Tomorrow I'll get you a case for it."

And so he had brought her that black purse, which she overburdened with keys to long-forgotten doors, a pair of scissors, and medications long past their expiration dates. She also threw in a smooth stone she'd picked up on the road. For days she was at a loss as to just how to carry it under her arm, and finally she settled on imitating the other women she saw on the streets. Sometimes she forgot it at home with the phone inside it, but eventually she got used to it and it became the crowning symbol of that femininity of hers that had returned to her ever since she decided to stop getting pregnant. Now if she left the house without it, she felt like something was missing.

She wipes her tears and continues down that road she used to walk with her mother. She crosses into a little alley behind the fire station where the men with their shiny copper helmets are still playing cards on a wooden box, waiting for an emergency alarm to sound so they can rush to the scene. She slips between the cars parked along the sidewalk, where the cassette tape vendors blare popular songs to high heaven and the shoeshines ogle the shoes of the passersby. She avoids walking in front of the men's cafés, where the men puff on the water pipes they lit up at the crack of dawn. She finds the cemetery gates open and goes in.

She sits for a few moments, wishing she could rest there for hours, all alone, on the stone bench under the shade of the tall eucalyptus tree. Voices can be heard coming from behind the grove. A couple of vagrants sharing a conversation. Most likely they'd spent the night there. They were denouncing the acts of some bearded youths who'd broken some grave markers with sledge hammers and knocked them to the ground. The vendor selling colorful prayer beads passes in front of her, guiding the blind lottery ticket seller in front of him. They were taking a shortcut through the cemetery. Two young lovers walking hand-in-hand disappear down a walkway and come back around on a different path, lost in the maze or maybe trying to take advantage of the chance to hold hands as long as possible before heading back out to the main street and the scrutiny of people's eyes. If only she could stay there, her mind free of worry, until nightfall. Her mother and father are not buried here. They're over on the north side of the city. They had argued in front of her about where her father would be buried. They didn't have a place in the city cemetery, nor in the villages they had come from, either—the villages had forgotten them and they the villages. The only option was to bury him in the Ghurabaa' Cemetery, the cemetery for strangers. Eventually, her mother joined him there, too.

A light, refreshing rain begins to fall again, so she walks quickly to the door leading to the banking district. A small line has developed in front of the bank tellers' windows, mostly workers drawing their salaries. She keeps walking, onto wider sidewalks, where the number of pedestrians dwindles and the number of unveiled women increases, many wearing high heels and tight jackets and trousers showing the outlines of their figures. A police car, its siren blaring to clear the traffic, escorts a caravan of military vehicles. The tires are covered with a thick layer of mud, and they all have their headlights on in broad daylight. The soldier sitting up front next to the driver of the first truck is fast asleep from exhaustion, his head propped on his hand.

There are two clean streets before her, with a row of ficus trees down the median. The woman working at one of the shops is standing in the display window dressing the naked wooden mannequins in the latest fashions. She adjusts them and then goes outside to the sidewalk to take a look before coming back inside to tighten the neckline which she'd found to be a bit too loose. Intisar crosses between the four-wheel drive vehicles to the other side of the street and arrives at her employer's house. She opens the main door, crosses through the little courtyard, and reaches the kitchen. She puts her purse down and searches for a rag. She wets it and goes outside to polish the copper plaque stuck to the post to the right of the front door. It had mud on it from the recent storm and was covered with fingerprints. She polishes it well, making the old, reddish copper shine like new, along with the phrase engraved on it that reads:

Al-Mulk Lillaah—Dominion Belongs to God Alone
Abdallah Azzam Residence

The owner had built the house out of stones from the old Ottoman Sérail administrative building after they decided to tear it down, and Intisar had inherited the job of cleaning it from her mother, Imm Mahmoud, who had come into it by way of her husband Husein al-Omar's sacrifice in the service of Mustapha Azzam, the grandfather. An excitable young man without work, Husein had volunteered to serve Mustapha Azzam in the beginning, just like that, in gratitude. Husein loved Mustapha Azzam because Mustapha loved people. He welcomed them into his home and looked after their needs, one by one. He served them from his heart. And so Husein would stand at attention at his door, waiting for him to head out on his daily rounds throughout the city. He'd walk behind Mustapha Azzam with a throng of bodyguards who watched the passersby with scrutiny, confirming the might of their *zaeem*, their boss. Like the others, Husein carried a cane with him, or kept a knife concealed in his jacket in case it became necessary. He later became friends with Azzam's personal chauffeur and started sitting beside him in the car whenever Mustapha Azzam himself was riding in the backseat, up until the time they got ambushed. They had deposited the Bey at his friend's house and set out on a nearby errand when gunfire rained down on them. Husein al-Omar took a bullet to his mouth, but the driver, who'd also been hit in both his hands, saved them from certain death by continuing to drive using his teeth. He somehow managed to get the car out of the range of the shooters, who thought they had hit their target: Mustapha Azzam.

"You faced death for my sake," the Bey said in gratitude when he went to see them in the hospital and gave them a sum of money, on top of paying their hospital fees. And in this way, the relationship between the newcomer to the city, Husein al-Omar (aka "Abu Mahmoud"), and the great Azzam family was forged.

His wife also joined the household of the Bey's son Abdallah and served them until her death. She shopped, cooked, and cleaned for them, babysat the children, and inherited their hand-me-down clothes and shoes for her own children to wear. They were all gone from this world now. The house was empty. Abdallah Bey's wife went to live with her daughter in Saudi Arabia, and Abdelkarim, the only son, left the country for France for many years before returning suddenly, which was when Intisar resumed taking care of the house. She made the journey across the city from the American Quarter every day, arriving before Abdelkarim woke up in the morning. He was a peculiar sort even as a child, and had become even more so after his long absence. He was *sensitive*. She was afraid *for* him, but not *of* him.

She locks the front gate and starts picking up the papers, shopping bags, and empty cigarette packs that passersby have tossed over the fence into the front yard, in a spiteful gesture aimed at the huge house concealed from their view behind the wall. In the past, one could peer in and catch a glimpse of the balcony and the entrance, but the dense ficus trees that had been planted one beside the other had grown and all their branches and thick evergreen leaves created a barrier behind the iron fence, effectively cutting off the Abdallah Azzam "Residence" from prying eyes, as well.

She goes back to the kitchen. She doesn't hear any movement and doesn't make any noise herself. She removes her headscarf. She runs her fingers through her thick black hair in front of the mirror hanging over the sink. The Azzam family's kitchen is her only place of rest and refuge, as long as Abdelkarim Bey is still asleep. It's the place where she can escape her life. She looks up through the wide window at the square patch of cloudy sky in the space between the buildings that have sprung up all around the house in every direction. She takes off her shoes and goes about her work in barefooted comfort. She opens the window in the formal living room to air it out from the odors of the night, wine and such things. She sweeps up the cigarette butts, picks up the mess in the bathroom, stacks the magazines neatly, and picks up the pillows strewn all over the floor. Next she turns off the television that was left on all night. Intisar always arrives before noon, finding Abdelkarim alone and quiet, and he stays alone and quiet until she leaves at sunset. All the rest occurs between early evening and dawn. The concierge of the building next door told her about some loud noise coming from the house at night. It sounded like voices shouting back and forth at each other, and the neighbors were complaining about it. She assured him that it wasn't shouting they were hearing, but *songs*.

"Songs?"

The doorkeeper's wife was unconvinced. She had been peering out from behind him to see if her husband, whom she'd noticed couldn't keep his eyes off Intisar when she passed by every morning, was being overly friendly with her now.

"More like the throes of death!"

Intisar shrugged off the notion with a brush of her hand and continued on her way. The concierge's wife, who had little faith in Intisar's virtue, whispered slyly to her husband, "How can he live all by himself like that, without a woman?"

Intisar stuck up for him because she knows his songs. The coarse male voices and the screeching female voices were abrasive to her at first, but then she got used to the tunes and even looked forward to hearing them. One time she stayed on a bit past her usual leaving time, and Abdelkarim thought he was alone in the house. He locked the windows, drew the curtains, and unleashed his diva. Peeking in, Intisar could see him sprawled out on his father's armchair in the dim evening light, eyes closed, intoxicated. Then he straightened up, put his elbow on his knee, and propped his head on the palm of his hand. With his facial features pulled back tightly, he contemplated the picture of the beautiful ballet dancer that Intisar had helped him hang on the wall. His other hand waved around to the beat of the music, with so much excitement it seemed he would explode.

Around ten o'clock, he calls to her, "Intisar." Her heart leaps as it does every day whenever she hears her name spoken in a morning voice fraught with the excesses of the night before. She puts her headscarf back on and calmly starts her morning chores. It is chandelier dusting day. Standing up on a ladder, she wipes the two big chandeliers that adorn the Azzam residence parlor and which have been a source of pride to them ever since moving there from their old house in the city souks. She polishes them once a month, following an old tradition entrusted to her by her mother. She disassembles the pieces of crystal one by one, and unscrews all the little candlesticks. She wipes each one and holds it up to see it sparkle again in the light, before securing it back in place. She completes the process with great industry, using lots of rags so as not to dust the successive pieces with a dusty rag. Trying her best not to get dizzy standing up on the ladder, she goes about her cleaning while he sits on the other side of the room, near the window where the sunlight is creeping in. He drinks his coffee in an unending series of sips, leaning over one of the trees he brought back from Paris in his suitcase.

Bonsai.

He had told Intisar the tree's name, and instructed her to water it with clean drinking water that had been boiled first and allowed to sit for twenty-four hours. He keeps a close eye on the leaves, binding the weak ones with metal twine. All one can hear in the house is soft opera music, disturbed from time to time by the sound of the crystal chandelier pendants knocking against each other, or of the scissor blades snipping at the little branches of the Chinese tea tree.

A long silence is broken by the sound of Quranic verses again.

"Lord, we believe in that Thou hast sent down, and we follow the Messenger. Inscribe us therefore with those who bear witness."

It was coming from the kitchen, from her purse. She freezes in place, up on the ladder, and looks over at Abdelkarim who has a big grin on his face, having figured out that what he was hearing was none other than a cell phone ring tone.

The chanter stops. A contemplative pause between two verses.

"And they devised, and God devised, and God is the best of devisers."

She jumps down from the top step of the ladder all the way to the floor, stumbling a little before managing to stand on her feet. She limps toward the kitchen on her twisted ankle, and finally gets there, completely out of breath.

"...I will set thy followers above the unbelievers till the Resurrection Day..."

Even though the verse has been cut off, Intisar opens the door and goes outside shouting "Hello? Hello? Ismail?" at the top of her lungs. "Ismail, my darling?" Her voice is swallowed up by the sound of a huge backhoe passing by on the next road over.

Defeated, she comes back inside, fumbling with the phone screen. Silence finds its way back into the parlor of the Azzam residence; Abdelkarim doesn't make a sound, doesn't move. Ever since Ismail's disappearance, she'd thought about seeking his help. There wasn't a single problem her family didn't turn to the Azzam family for help with. Her brother the public school teacher, for example, was able to sue for every last lira of his monthly salary, even after his health had deteriorated and he was hospitalized and had stopped teaching completely. And when parliamentary elections heated up and enthusiastic supporters of this or that candidate bombarded her brother Mahmoud with their attempts to win him over, he was always the first to stand in the doorway of his shop and shout for all to hear with his hands raised in defiance of all their promises, "Honor is worth much more than money, and let those present inform those who are absent that we belong to the Azzams…"

On her way from the American Quarter, she always plans to raise the topic of Ismail with Abdelkarim. But she banishes the idea from her mind the moment she arrives and sees him waking up with his puffy morning face, and his dry throat, drinking the glass of water he always puts near his head when he goes to bed; or when she goes in to tidy up his bedroom and sees his sheets all crumpled up as if they'd been part of some major battle the night before, and finds drool stains on his pillows, mixed with red wine, and is forced to change the pillowcases on a daily basis. She changes them, taking time to adjust the corners and flatten them with her hand and smooth out any lumps, her heart pounding all the while for fear he might see her touching his pillowcases.

Abdelkarim had changed, too. For some time now, he'd withdrawn from her, as if the day she gave in to Ismail's wishes and came to the house wearing that coarse brown baggy robe, he suddenly didn't see her anymore. As if he'd boycotted her. A curtain dropped between them. Before that, starting right after he'd come back from Paris, he used to sit with her in the kitchen, and together they would finish distilling orange blossom water in the little still he'd bought after consulting with his aunt. The previous April, he and Intisar had plucked the blossoms together from the four remaining bitter orange trees out in the garden. During that time, Intisar would come back to the American Quarter each evening with her clothes infused with the fragrance of orange blossoms. And out of a feeling of nostalgia that developed in Abdelkarim during his time in Paris, he liked to make the local traditional sweets of his city, like *Halawit al-Rizz,* and Intisar would dust her own hands and his hands with flour and powdered sugar as they kneaded the rice dough and rolled it into sheets. Then together they would taste and eat what they had made, standing in front of the kitchen window. Afterward, he would withdraw to the family piano he was always complaining needed tuning, while she went off to do the dishwashing and laundry.

She decides not to go back up on the ladder to clean the chandeliers, afraid of falling from the top step. She sits there, incapable of performing her housecleaning chores, huffing and puffing in the hope he'll notice, but he doesn't lift his eyes from the bonsai tree. He takes out a syringe and draws some yellow liquid from a little vial that looks just like the vial the nurse at Rahme Clinic had waved in the air as she drew penicillin out of it while a very young Intisar shut her eyes to avoid seeing the nurse stick the needle in her mother Umm Mahmoud's flabby white thigh. Abdelkarim's hand trembles a little as he carefully tries to stick the needle into the tree's slender trunk. She observes him, and postpones seeking his help until he finishes his little operation, but he doesn't put the syringe down until he's finished misting and shining all those little green leaves that never wilt. Holding her head between her hands, Intisar looks down at the bits of nail polish still left on her toenails. She presses down on her knees to stop them from shaking and then forces herself to action.

"It's my eldest son, Bey…"

He does not realize she is speaking to him, so she pulls herself together, walks over to him, and pointing to the cellphone in her hand she says, "It's Ismail!"

"What's wrong with him?"

"They took him."

"Where?"

"I don't know. This phone, it rings but I don't hear my son's voice. I'm really worried about him!"

"Ismail is my only support," she adds after a brief hesitation, choking on her words.

She lowers her head. "He loves you very much, Bey," she continues. "After he stopped coming here, he always asked about your health…"

"…and your trees!" she adds, embarrassed. "He never forgets your conversations and always says what a wonderful person you are."

Abdelkarim motions for Intisar to come closer and hand him the cell phone.

It's a Nokia 8890 in a bright red plastic case. The simplest and cheapest of its kind. He asks her what the phone number is, but she doesn't know what he means and simply answers "No." He checks to see what is stored in the phone and finds it to be empty except for "Missed Calls." There's just one number that has been recorded, with numerous attempts, along with the date and time of each attempt. All of the calls had come in in the last twenty-four hours. It was an international number beginning with 00964. Abdelkarim takes the number down on a slip of paper, not really knowing what he can possibly do to help find Ismail. "I'll try my best," he says, handing back the phone.

Intisar finishes up her day. She prepares meals according to Abdelkarim's tastes, and puts in a load of her children's dirty laundry, which she sometimes carries with her to the Azzam house and then carries all the way back to the American Quarter nice and clean at the end of the day. She tries to pick the ripe persimmon fruits before they rot on the tree there in the garden, but she can't reach them. She walks the perimeter of the house, taking down the advertisements and obituary notices that get posted on the outer walls on a daily basis. She has a special wide knife for that purpose. At sunset, she locks the front door behind her and heads back the way she came, following her mother's old route for good luck.

Night falls suddenly, and the city falls into its daily slumber. The souk streets are completely dark. The municipality security guards of her youth no longer walk the streets at night, checking the padlocks on the shop doors, making their rounds again and again to make sure no one tampers with them, and blowing their whistles from time to time to signal to each other that their beat is clear. Something in the atmosphere has changed. A feeling of anxiety keeps nagging at her, a feeling that some danger is about to befall her that she has refused to acknowledge. True, no one had ever tried to hurt her or make a pass at her, and none of the men passing by ever said anything improper to her. But on hearing the sound of footsteps coming from the souks in the dark, she'd begun to look around cautiously. She'd slow down or stop in front of a store window that was still lit up at this late hour, and wait until the man walking behind her passed her, without looking him in the face, before continuing on her way. She was barely ten years old when her mother had started sending her by herself to pick up the *balila,* a boiled chickpea dish, for the family's lunch from the *foule* stand near the Gold Souks. The fava bean vendor would make a note in his ledger instead of taking money from her, because her father would square the bill when he passed by a bit later to eat some *foule bitahini.* As she crossed the bridge on the way back home, she would open the edge of the container and sneak a few hot chickpeas to curb her hunger before bringing it home.

She knows everything by heart, every door and every narrow passageway where she rendezvoused with teenage boys in her youth. She could walk it with her eyes closed. She says hello to the coppersmith, meanders over to the bakery and to the pharmacy. Some of the vendors call her "Imm Ismail" and give her good prices. But now there had come to be more and more strangers in the souks, faces she'd never seen before. Many were squatters living in some nearby abandoned houses who roamed the streets at night, making her nervous and unable to relax until she reached the other side of the river where she began her trek up the steps leading to her house in the American Quarter.

As she approaches the house, she can hear some commotion coming from inside, laughter and voices out of place at this late hour. Her heart starts pounding. Maybe Ismail has come back and they are celebrating his return! No, it's something else. It seems the shocking reality of two families living together under the same roof of one cramped and crumbling house had drawn the attention of a journalist from one of the TV stations. She'd been impressed by repeated references to the widespread despair infecting the city's old neighborhoods and its connection to the surge in violence and fundamentalist movements in the area. All the inhabitants of both floors of the cramped house, and all the neighbors as well, had congregated in the entryway to watch the interview that the journalist with the pretty face and short stature, which was quite different from how she appeared on camera, had informed them would be aired at the end of the eight o'clock news. The grown-ups were contradicting all the comments made by the journalist who appeared to be taken in by every detail of the scene. And everyone squealed with joy when Bilal Muhsin's youngest son appeared on the screen, leaning against the wall as he made his way down the stairs with difficulty. Their eyes darted back and forth between the stairs on the TV screen and the actual stairs right there in front of them. Their voices mingled with al-Mashnouq's wife's voice, who could be heard introducing her children to the viewers and pointing out their sleeping quarters. In the meantime, the cameraman zooms in on some water stains on the wall from the recent rainstorm, and the series of clips ends to the accompaniment of a long round of applause from the audience before they head back home with the image of al-Mashnouq himself dressed in an *abaya* robe he'd put on just for the occasion, sitting in his armchair with a big smile on his face, watching his favorite shows on the television.

In the middle of the night, while Intisar Muhsin tosses and turns in her bed and pleads with her little daughter Ahlam to go to sleep, Abdelkarim Azzam sits all alone, enjoying his boisterous nightly routine of loud music, while his attention to the picture of the ballet dancer with the bereaved look in her eyes is interrupted intermittently by long sips from glasses of single malt whiskey he's mixed with a splash of water, and which hold the promise of bringing him sleep, something he knows will not come to him before dawn. In the midst of all this, he tries over and over again to call the number he jotted down from Intisar's cell phone. He dials the number on his home phone, which had been one of the first land lines ever to be installed in the city, and doesn't get anywhere with the first ten attempts. All he gets is a busy signal. Giving it one last try, he finally gets through. The phone starts ringing on the other end and someone picks up. Abdelkarim speaks, but no one answers.

2

Abdelkarim had caught his first glimpse of the American Quarter through one of the battlements of the Crusader castle. He was with his sister at the castle, at the tail end of an outing, during which his father had entrusted them to a tour guide who looked like a police officer in his navy blue cap, khaki uniform, and shiny shoes. He wanted the guide to acquaint them with the "downtown," as he called the city. They toured for an entire day, like foreigners, stopping in front of the *tarbush* hatmaker in Khan al-Khayyateen, the Tailors' Bazaar, and at one point they ran into a crowd of demonstrators passing out flyers, led by an angry young man wearing a Palestinian *kufiyah* scarf who was rallying the crowd. They walked past the Mansouri Great Mosque but didn't go inside because of the protesters. With their little legs having grown tired from the climb, Abdelkarim and his sister reached the highest walls of the citadel, which had been built by Count Raymond de Toulouse out of sandstone, thanks to donations from Christian pilgrims, after he'd given up all hope of gaining jurisdiction over Jerusalem. The two had gotten bored with the series of cold halls where Queen Marguerite de Provence had resided with her entourage in 1250. These were all names that the tour guide-policeman pronounced in a perfect French accent while waving his baton in the air. Abdelkarim did not stop to look at anything, except for the small cannon, which the people stuffed with gunpowder and fired off every evening during the month of Ramadan, the loud bang signaling the start of *Iftar*. In an effort to relieve his boredom and exhaustion, he was about to start asking to go home when his sister suddenly shouted, "Look! Over there! Imm Mahmoud's house..."

She was pointing across the way with great urgency, like a sailor looking out on the horizon and shouting that he's spotted dry land. The guide gave in to their game, and Abdelkarim rushed over to one of the openings in the citadel wall overlooking the river. Suddenly the American Quarter came into his view, like a colorful picture inside a stone frame: heaps of houses stuck together, blocking the horizon; balconies filled with colorful laundry hanging on clotheslines; flocks of pigeons circling the clear sky; and a giant, dense tree with its thick branches that had battled a very long time to live and grow and finally explode, all alone, in a spring burst of lilac in the midst of a forest of cement and stone.

The moment he got out of bed the next morning, Abdelkarim rushed to the kitchen to tell Imm Mahmoud that he knew where she lived and had seen her house. She promised to take him to see the American Quarter in person. She waited for a day when Abdelkarim was out of school and didn't have homework, and she also took advantage of his mother's having gone to visit a relative in the hospital in Beirut, to ask permission from his father Abdallah Bey al-Azzam, appealing to the *affection* he had for her that had been passed down through generations. He was wearing his satin robe over his clothes and was sitting in his *Louis Quinze* armchair—which probably no one else in the world ever sat in while Abdallah Bey was still alive—while listening to the radio that he had turned up to a much higher volume than usual.

He quieted Imm Mahmoud with a signal of his finger, not allowing her to move until the end of Umm Kulthoum's song, "Al-Qalb ya'shaq kull jamil" (The heart loves every beautiful thing), which was airing for the first time on Cairo Broadcasting Station. Imm Mahmoud stood beside the door, listening with a level of attention she thought would please Abdallah Bey who was floating in a state of bliss, somewhere between tears and joy; surely he would not be able to refuse a request from her while in this state. Once he'd drunk his fill of Umm Kulthoum, he nodded his head, allowing Abdelkarim to visit the American Quarter, and was content to merely remind Imm Mahmoud she must take the driver with them.

Imm Mahmoud sat on the edge of the seat, not wanting to allow the weight of her body to sink too deeply into the sweet-smelling black leather. Abdelkarim, on the other hand, sat up front, burning with anticipation for their arrival, and urged Hasan al-Owayk to speed up, though Hasan didn't dare. He drove through the crowded narrow streets, mumbling to himself, annoyed by the fact that a luxury car such as the one he was driving—a Jaguar E Type current year model 1972 that Abdallah Bey had yet to succeed in crowning with a blue Parliament Member license plate, and probably never would—was not designed to be driven down those narrow and crumbling roads. Hasan's heightened cautiousness culminated in his decision not to accompany them, preferring instead to look after the car, which he parked near the vegetable souk at the bottom of the quarter for fear one of the neighborhood kids would scratch its shiny sky-blue paint. However, he didn't last long before nodding off as he sat there at the wheel waiting for their return.

Abdelkarim began the long climb up the steps, walking beside Imm Mahmoud, who had told the neighbors about the imminent visit of the grandson of Mustapha al-Azzam to the American Quarter. With the thrill of the initial discovery still fresh in his mind, Abdelkarim trained his sight on the Crusader Castle, searching for the battlement from where he'd peered down at the quarter just a few days earlier. Soon he began drawing the attention of the neighborhood kids who had just finished the project of taking apart a naked and hairless doll they'd found tossed on the ground and distributing the plastic body parts among themselves. As they followed him up the steps, they whispered his name to each other—close buddies walking two by two with arms draped over shoulders and staring awestruck at this person who had suddenly appeared before them: a miniature man Imm Mahmoud had intentionally dressed in the very best clothes hanging in his closet. The outfit had been a gift from his uncle who often traveled in and out of various European cities. It was a complete replica of what the children of rich Englishmen would wear when they went hunting or horseback riding: a golfing suit, with suspenders to hold up the trousers that reached the knees, followed by long stockings with a checkered pattern, a white shirt, bow tie, tight shoes, plus a soft cap made from the same fabric as the suit. Abdelkarim thought the neighborhood kids were just walking on their way, as usual, until two broad-shouldered youths appeared at the top of the steps. They were carrying a skinny old man who looked half-asleep and was sitting on a chair, clearing a path calling out, "*Dastoor, dastoor*, make way..." as they descended the stairs. They were taking the old man to the riverbank. Abdelkarim stared at them in disbelief, and when the boys got too far for him to continue watching this strange cargo, he noticed that the neighborhood kids had been staring at him, and not at the old man swaying in the air like a ragdoll. That was something they were used to seeing on a daily basis. They carried him that way so he could get an hour of sunshine and enjoy watching the vendors and the passersby.

As soon as they got there, Imm Mahmoud asked for Intisar, her youngest daughter who was about the same age as Abdelkarim. She told her oldest son Mahmoud to go fetch her as quickly as possible from wherever she might be, and then complained about her and her devilish antics. That was how Abdelkarim heard about Intisar before ever seeing her. Her companionship was the only kind of entertainment Imm Mahmoud could offer him beyond the glass of *jallab* fruit syrup over shaved ice she immediately treated him to after showing him to the best seat in the formal living room, the rose-colored sofa whose expensive velvet fabric had started to wear off here and there. Some neighborhood kids who'd managed to sneak into the house gathered in a circle around him, benefitting from the various fruits and treats Imm Mahmoud served to her boss's son, after which they quickly forgot the reason they'd come inside to begin with and started snickering secretively among themselves. When Mahmoud returned with Intisar in tow, they didn't even notice. He had her by the shoulder to keep her from fleeing from him as she had done a few minutes earlier, forcing him to chase after her.

A very angry and reluctant little Intisar entered the house, shyly hiding her face in her brother's clothing as he escorted her to the empty seat her mother had left for her beside Abdelkarim. She lowered her head and kept her eyes shut. She didn't turn in Abdelkarim's direction and didn't answer him either when he asked her where she had been, but rather shrugged her shoulders in protest at having been stopped from playing. When she finally yielded to her situation, she stole a peek at the boy sitting beside her out of the corner of her eye and noticed his strange outfit and shiny hair slicked back with Brylcreem. Without any sort of introductions, she moved closer to him and whispered in his ear to let her take the cap he had respectfully taken off his head. He promised to take her for a ride down to the sea in his father's car, and in return she pulled her hand out from behind her back, where she'd been hiding it since she came in, and gave him a big, red, shiny candy apple. Abdelkarim looked around at the others and hesitated before taking the apple by the stick. He examined it carefully with his eyes and then brought it to his mouth. But Intisar stopped him, warning him not to bite into it but just lick it instead, because they were going to share it between the two of them. The other children started to laugh and Abdelkarim got very confused as he continued eyeing the candy apple, but Imm Mahmoud came to his rescue. She pushed Intisar back away from him and gave him the candy apple to have all for himself, though it had gotten a bit dusty by this time. He put it away and when Imm Mahmoud took him back down to the car, he pulled it out and licked it and bit into it in a hurry so he could finish it before he got home. And that was how Abdelkarim al-Azzam returned from his first trip ever to the American Quarter: dressed up in his strange English suit, his lips red with dye from the candy apple that looked more like lipstick stains left by some woman's haphazard kiss.

He craved those candy apples a lot. And he secretly yearned for them, especially after he asked his mother for one and she got all upset and started mocking the way the candy apple maker dipped the apples in colored syrup and left them out for flies to hover around all day long. "Why would you want such a thing?" she asked haughtily, not comprehending how her son could turn his nose up at the *Halawit al-Jibn* sweet cheese dessert that they special ordered in shredded *mshabshaleh* style from the best sweet makers in Rifa'i Hill and instead had his heart set on this pauper's sweet he saw lined up on the tray of the emaciated vendor who stood there straight as an arrow every morning on the corner of *Shari' al-Maktabat,* Bookstore Row. Bright red, no matter what the season, and right next to them was a rack of brightly colored "bird candies" children would whistle through until they got tired of whistling and transitioned to eating them in chunks or sucking on them and letting them melt slowly in their mouths.

He yearned for everything he saw through the window of the school bus they registered him to ride once he got strong enough and his father decided he should mix with his peers. After that, Hasan al-Owayk no longer drove him to school in the Jaguar, or opened the door for him, or escorted him into the building through the teachers' entrance while carrying his heavy book bag for him. When Abdelkarim would climb up onto the school bus, nearly all the seats would be empty, because the driver started his route out at the farthest stops first, starting with the new houses amid the orange groves and then heading toward the school located across from the old souks. He would choose a seat next to a window and could hear his heartbeat speed up as they approached the wall of the nuns' school with the buildings behind it that the Italians had transformed into a hospital during World War II. He hoped to see the two blonde French girls walking to school from their nearby house, the older one holding a white umbrella over both of them on rainy mornings. Oh, if only he could hear what the giggling younger one was whispering into her older sister's ear as they made their way to that splendid kingdom of theirs that he could never enter. He would always be in exile from those two, behind the windows of the school bus as it got washed by the rain. A lump would form in his throat as he looked longingly at their ponytails dancing in the air. Their colorful hair ribbons were the talk of the town; they had a different color for each day of the week. They always wore their striped school uniforms, but one time he'd seen them wearing simple, brightly colored dresses that showed their pale white arms and a bit of their shoulders. And on that hot day, on account of his exaggerated stares, he thought maybe the older sister finally noticed him, and when she cast two quick glances at him, he wasn't sure if she was looking at him out of curiosity or attraction. So he became torn not knowing if he should content himself with these occasional opportunities to look at them, while his life and theirs never crossed paths despite their living in an apartment that was just a few short minutes away from his own house, or if he should create some occasion to meet them close up. He could ask his sister if she knew them and then have her invite them to her next birthday party, for example, rather than her girlfriends with the pimples all over their faces or the ones wearing those metal braces the dentists were so fond of recommending every chance they got. However, just as he was beginning to come up with a plan toward this end, he quickly realized that he really wanted to meet both sisters together, and if they were to be separated, the whole notion would lose its luster, and then, in any case, he'd be at a total loss as to what to say to them.

Nothing could console him from the bewitching sight of those two in the morning and his feeling of estrangement from their unreachable world except when the school bus, which had started to fill up with lots of other boys, reached the center of the city that was struggling to wake from its slumber. From there, they would head down the nearby street where all the movie theatres were and where the driver would be forced to slow down or even stop sometimes due to traffic. This gave the school children a good stretch of time to look at all the posters and make plans to come back during the weekend to see the movies. Some of the boys would secretly point out to each other the entrance to the Mu'tam Building, whispering that it led to a "cabaret" where you would be greeted by *"artistes"* after ten o'clock at night. And they also knew that they secretly showed dirty movies in the small theatre on the bottom floor. The kids would come back during the weekend, all except Abdelkarim, who was forbidden from going to such movie theatres to sit in the dark all by himself, thanks to his father's firm conviction that the cinema had become nothing but a hotbed for punks hooting and hollering obscenities. Abdelkarim had grown envious of people he sometimes saw on his way back from school around four-thirty in the afternoon, whether he knew them or not. They'd be coming out from the movie theatre, their eyes squinting from sudden exposure to sunlight after having had their fill of Gina Lollobrigida in *Buona Sera, Mrs. Campbell*, or the magnetism of Gregory Peck in *Shoot Out*. If they were feeling hungry, they would meander over to the nearby *moghrabiyyeh* couscous vendor and walk away with a pita wrap stuffed with hot couscous that had been scooped right out of the massive copper pot whose burner was always lit.

Abdelkarim was a highly envied and heavily protected child. His grandfather Mustapha's reputation preceded him, as did the statue of him holding the national declaration of independence in his right hand, which had stood for many long years at the entrance to the city. The day they unveiled the statue, Abdelkarim had been seated in a chair in the front row, his legs not long enough to touch the ground, surrounded by volunteer attendants holding black umbrellas over the heads of the Parliament Ministers who were drenched with sweat in their official uniforms. The curtain got stuck when they attempted to pull the cord and let it drop, and so a young man jumped up and was able to slide the white fabric off of Mustapha al-Azzam's stern face looking toward the sea. Of course, their political opponents criticized them for allowing to have their father standing with his back turned to the city. When a poet took the stage, Abdelkarim was frightened by all the clapping and shouting that ensued when he raised his long and crooked index finger into the air and shouted, "You live long, while the tyrants' years are numbered!" It was the opening to a poem in which he crowned in words the family patriarch who, according to historical documents, traced his heritage to Tannoukh bin Qahtan bin Aouf bin Kinda bin Jandab bin Madhhaj bin Sa'ad bin Tayy bin Tamim bin al-Mundhir bin Maa' as-Samaa', as circulated by the celebration's sponsor. After the speeches, the dignitaries who had come from the capital for the special occasion were treated to a banquet of fresh seafood at *Al-Shati' al-Fiddi,* Silver Shore Restaurant, at the beginning of which Abdelkarim managed to spill squid ink onto his white shirt, causing him to rush off on foot. He walked by himself with the black stains on his shirt all the way home, where they found him, after following the trail to his bedroom, stretched out on his bed, head buried in his pillow, which is how he remained until the next morning, refusing every plea for him to change into his pajamas or take his shoes off at the very least.

The *Raa'iyya* poem, where every line ends with the letter *raa',* by the revolutionary poet from Aleppo was transformed into a family jewel when one of the local newspapers published it in booklet form and distributed a thousand free copies to passersby and café patrons. And a local calligrapher copied it in gilded Kufi script, mounted it in a huge frame, and attached it to the trunk of a big tree in one of the public squares. Abdallah Bey knew it by heart, despite its length. He would sit Abdelkarim on his healthy knee and recite to his pupil those lines glorifying his grandfather that seemed to have been written about a stranger, and then together they would leaf through the pages of the thick photo album as

Abdallah taught his son the names that went with all the faces.

"This is your grandfather!" he'd say, pointing to a picture of Mustapha al-Azzam disembarking a train in Alexandria, saluting back at his greeters, some of whom were dressed in military garb.

"And who is this?"

"That's you!" little Abdelkarim would answer, standing on one foot and reaching out to touch his father's face and trace his nose and cheeks, making sure he and the radiant young man standing behind a semicircle of men seated in wicker chairs in the picture, were one and the same. At first Abdelkarim wasn't always able to identify his grandfather correctly, due to all the different types of uniforms he was pictured wearing during various time periods. These were old photographs and some of the details had become blurry over time. In some he was pictured with a mufti's turban on his head, which he began wearing at the age of eighteen as the youngest mufti under the Ottoman Sultanate. He'd inherited it from his father, who had taken it from his father who had left it to pursue politics. Sometimes he was pictured wearing a *tarbush* while standing on the podium of honor at an Independence Day celebration in Burj Square in the capitol, and other times he had on an American cap while in the company of government ministers and foreign ambassadors, or sometimes he was bareheaded with his blond curly hair flying in the wind. But always, in all of the shots, whether he was prepared and posed for them or in the rare ones when the photographer's lens caught him unawares, however he was standing and no matter what outfit he was wearing, he always had a noticeable look of displeasure in his eyes—the distress of having just been informed of some injurious accident or the death of someone dear. It was a look of disdain that never left him and which was transformed in the pictures of his second son Abdallah into a mixture of something between dejection and boredom. A curse on the world came from those honey-colored eyes, though it went unnoticed by little Abdelkarim who was more than excited to be vying with his father to flip to the next page in the photo album and reach the last and most recent picture—the statue of Mustapha al-Azzam in the middle of the roundabout while cars circled around it in every direction.

Abdallah Bey became the family's memory keeper after he yielded to the 'eldest-son rule,' which sent his brother into Parliament, and after a bullet shattered his right kneecap. It was said he'd been shot by one of his family's adversaries in the city souks. He was forced to go through the rest of his life with a cane, and suffered aches and pains during the cold months. He'd clench his teeth or bite his lip whenever he rose to shake hands with people who still remembered him at various occasions. He made every effort to stand up for every visitor, and each one in his turn congratulated him while insisting he should not trouble himself to get up. And on these occasions during holidays and such, Abdelkarim got his fill of kisses from his auntie and his mother's aging girlfriends. He sat politely, watching without listening to people who seemed to have been born wearing suits and neckties, and religious clerics who never got tired of repeating Quranic verses and proverbs one could not possibly refute. Nothing ignited their conversations better than news and stories about the grand families, about blood ties and relations by marriage. A favorite topic involved presenting evidence against plagiarists who had changed their names in an attempt to enter into the golden register of well-known families. They were on to them, despite their having made the name changes three or four generations earlier. Inevitably, one of the supporters would volunteer to recite once again the story that everyone knew by heart about the day when Mustapha al-Azzam, suddenly confronted by a French officer with his revolver drawn and surrounded by Senegalese soldiers armed with bayonets, ripped his shirt open, bared his chest, and shouted in French, "Go ahead and shoot!"

There was never an Eid Fitr holiday feast ending the Ramadan fast that passed without Abdelkarim getting a new suit. The tailor would come to the house to take his measurements, and eventually Abdelkarim would come outside for a little stroll with his cousin Riyad who was two years older than Abdelkarim and was always trying to impose his higher rank on him. Riyad would puff himself up as he walked, hold his shoulders high, and make a point of being first to return the greetings of passersby. He was always one step ahead of Abdelkarim as they strutted down the sidewalk on Azmi Bey Street with their hands in their pockets. They'd get almost all the way to the end of the street before their bodyguard caught up with them and brought them back home, following orders. It seemed exposing the Azzam boys to public scrutiny for too long was not desirable. They would come back home full of disappointment, having left the street an open arena for the boys who smoked Marlboros and gathered in a circle around the espresso seller, reading newspapers and making secretive remarks at the girls who slowed down in front of shop windows to look at the latest fashions—remarks that might lead to a rendezvous and some stolen touches over dishes of ice cream in a dark corner of one of the new sweet shops.

His mother would feel sorry for him seeing him so gloomy and not uttering a word. And so she would ask the driver to take him for a little trip into the city. Hasan al-Owayk would take him to a street filled with an unbelievable crowd of boys who'd waited in a long line the night before at the neighborhood barber shop and stayed up all night at the tailor shop while the final buttons were sewn onto their new suits. They bathed after their mothers scrubbed their scalps with olive oil soap, and they went to bed smelling the aroma of dyed leather coming from the new shoes they'd placed close to their pillows. They'd woken up early and hovered around their uncles thinking of nothing but taking off the moment one of them gave them some Eid money. Then they'd go off in groups, spilling over the sidewalks into the middle of the road. They bantered and joked while a throng of cotton candy and *nammoura* semolina cake vendors trailed behind them. The younger cousin contented himself with the swings or with piling with a mob of his peers onto a mini truck that took them on a little ride to the seacoast and back. They sang out their children's rhymes at the top of their lungs, and then they cried when their older siblings with their teenage buddies refused to let them do dangerous bicycle tricks with them in the wide city streets. Large groups of them came down from the American Quarter and other poor neighborhoods crouched over the city's river. They invaded the squares and the streets for two or three days, with their new haircuts or with spots of bright dye in their hair. Their numbers swelled even more with children from the nearby Palestinian refugee camp who were driven in by taxis in waves. Together they explored every corner of the city where, during the remainder of the year, they had no business being there. They felt invincible, knowing they were carrying sharp knives in their pockets, ready to cut down any adversaries if a fight broke out, the inevitable finishing touch of every holiday. They stole falafel balls from the edge of the vendor carts despite the vendors' scolding them as they swam in a fog of deep-fryer oil and the scent of pickles. They tried their luck at three-card poker and the thimble game. They picked little square cards with girls' names on them—Nour al-Huda, Abir, or Sahar—and they won packs of American cigarettes that they divided among themselves. They blew into colorful calibrated water pipes. They paid a lira to look at pictures of actresses through a looking glass. They ate *baraziq*, sesame cookies, and filled up on salty red pickled turnips that unlocked their appetites for the holiday *ma'moul,* stuffed shortbread cookies. Rich for a day, they flexed their tattooed muscles and conquered the city on this special free-for-all day.

Abdelkarim al-Azzam watched them from inside the Jaguar as it slowly rolled along, to the rhythm of the pedestrians walking down the middle of the street who were in no hurry to move out of the way of cars. Hasan al-Owayk never honked his horn at the happy children celebrating the holiday, until one day when he found himself surrounded by a rowdy mob of them. He realized the danger Abdelkarim Bey was in when he heard their fists pounding the trunk of the car, even though Abdelkarim seemed delighted by the procession—especially when he smiled and waved to them and they got all excited and pounded on the car twice as much. They surrounded the car from three sides and started dancing around and shouting about lifting the car up while pushing on it and setting it rocking up and down. This terrified al-Owayk, who waited for the first opportunity to turn down a side road to get away from them and shake off the ones clinging to the Jaguar's bumper. They all shouted in disapproval, and one of them threw a rock that shattered the rear window, sending shards of glass onto Abdelkarim's head. He had been wounded without realizing it. When Hasan noticed it in the rearview mirror he shrieked. He took Abdelkarim straight home with him to his wife who took care of the wound with some iodine and bandages. The two of them agreed on the story they would tell when they went together to talk to Abdelkarim's parents.

That is how, at a very young age, Abdelkarim started to develop the feeling that the world was somewhere he was *not.* It wasn't in the school his father insisted he should stay at, with the "Christian brothers." He wouldn't transfer him to the Dar al-Tarbiyah wa al-Talim al-Islamiyyah School, an institution established so Muslim children would not have to go on studying at foreign missionary schools. His father, Abdallah al-Azzam, whose own father had built an Andalusian-style palace, raised the Arab flag over it, and made it the winter headquarters for Emir Faisal's regime in Damascus before he was defeated by General Gouraud; his father, the leader of the famous strike calling for unity with Syria that lasted forty days, how could he be happy to have his only son attend morning mass at school with the Christians? Nothing broke up the monotony of lessons at that school except for a theatrical production chock full of put-on emotions, tight pants, and authentic French accents of Moliere's comedy, *L'Amour Médecin* (Dr. Cupid). Or maybe they would bring in a guest magician who could pull a dove out of his sleeve. Nothing rescued Abdelkarim from his boredom except the library, which he frequented on a daily basis after he volunteered to be his class representative. He would sit there all alone while his classmates got caught up in all their clamor during recess, to the point where the Frère in charge of the library gave him the key, after making sure he was a diligent boy who could be trusted. During those longs periods of time spent alone there with the books, the pains of adolescence plagued him. Obscure emotions, unwarranted despair, sometimes caused him to burst into tears and sob out loud. His sadness intermingled with his readings, and he would copy into his notebook Apollinaire's calligramme dedicated to the memory of his comrades entitled, "The Stabbed Dove and the Fountain of Water," or he'd write some of Mallarme's poetry in beautiful handwriting:

Alas, the flesh is weary, and I've read all the books

He would recite poems with eyes closed, fully engrossed, and he also adopted the poet's abstinence from sex—he who hadn't even gotten near a woman's body yet, except for Siranush, the Armenian piano teacher who gave him lessons on Saturday afternoons. He'd sit close beside her, brushing against her and feeling a kind of warmth and arousal of desire. His explications in French in response to literary questions were quoted among the teachers and the monks. They would read them to other classes, amazed that the grandson of the mufti of the Muslims was more proficient in their language than their own countrymen. At age sixteen, Abdelkarim believed he could grasp the meanings of cryptic poems and could crack their hidden symbols. He would recite them to himself with exaggeration and gesticulations, repeating the verses with tears in his eyes from the tenderness of the meanings, while stretched out on the porch swing at the entrance to his house, all alone, imagining himself sitting shoulder to shoulder with a band of decadent poets, sipping bitter absinthe from their glasses at the little Parisian cabaret as depicted in a painting by Fantin-Latour in the book on nineteenth-century French literature. Or he'd be dreaming of defiant, passionate women waiting for him in some European city that he always imagined drowning in a winter fog, which revealed, during brief moments of clarity, awe-inspiring stone edifices and cathedrals with walls adorned with pictures of saints speaking to birds and showing affection to lions while solemn organ music echoed all about.

He doesn't wake from his book dreaming until Imm Mahmoud suddenly appears before him, standing in the doorway, looking faint and pale, muttering inaudibly to herself. Abdelkarim gets up to help her but she manages to get control of herself somewhat. She has just arrived from the old city neighborhoods, with a look of terror on her face from what she saw there. She looks behind herself to make sure what she has just witnessed didn't follow her here, to the house of her employer.

The lady of the house comes out to see her and Imm Mahmoud tells her how she came upon some people gathered around two dead bodies that had been tossed into the river—two young men the river had washed up downstream at the point where the river shrinks to a little stream. They got lodged under the bridge, and there were dark splotches of blood on their clothing. Abdelkarim's mother slapped her thigh in dismay, and the maid went inside to tell her story once again to Abdallah Bey. Abdelkarim remained seated on the porch swing, reciting to himself with sorrowful and quiet compassion, the poem about the soldier, "The Sleeper in the Valley," bleeding from two red bullet holes in his chest. He evoked the poem, trying to find a place inside his literary daydreams to shroud the two casualties of the dried-up river.

However, this "poetic" phase of his didn't last long. Upon embarking on his third decade of life, his patience for delving into the meanings of things that remained stubbornly obscure, waned, and it appeared that his adolescent sensibility and those dark emotions had crept into him via the dampness of the school building, its dreariness, and its gloomy, emaciated trees. Later on, when meeting up with a classmate he hadn't seen in a very long time, he postulated during a moment of clarity, that during his long years of residence at the "Detention Camp" he must have contracted a sadness virus he carried and from which he would never be cured his whole life. It was a feeling of despair that cast a dark cloud over him from time to time, confining him to his house for days on end, during which he refused to receive any visitors. When it came, it would reawaken his parents' worries, especially after his mother ran into a friend of hers who suggested the term "melancholy" to describe some of his behavior as she attempted to analyze his condition. His mother reiterated the description to her husband, who felt he'd been dealt a heavy blow when he discovered that all the manifestations of a sudden breakdown that he had tried to ignore ever since he started noticing them in Abdelkarim were now smacking him right in the face. He feared that tendency toward depression that affected the Azzam family, generation after generation, passing over some while plaguing others, like those bouts of pessimism that hit him for no reason and with no warning, and his paternal aunt who'd passed it on to one of her daughters, forcing her to stay locked up in the house, smoking her water pipe, refusing to meet a single stranger or visitor until her death, and all the way back to his grandfather the mufti and the stories that circulated even to this day of his angry temperament and served as a kind of proverbial family example. All of a sudden, Abdallah al-Azzam dreaded the possibility that this trait had manifested itself in his only son, Abdelkarim.

Among the various pieces of advice suggested, there was an agreement of opinion in the family around the notion that marriage might cure him of his ailment. His sister had preceded him by getting married to a young Saudi fellow she'd met in one of her classes at the American University in Beirut. She went to live with him in his country. As a result, Abdelkarim's mother succeeded in persuading him to marry a girl whose father was raking in big profits from oil and gas imports. The celebration was a modest one, to the displeasure of the bride and her family, but things went along just fine, so it seemed, for a few months, until one day when the bride took her mother-in-law aside to complain about Abdelkarim. He had only come near her three times—once on the wedding night and then two other times when he was dead drunk. He didn't even look at her anymore. If she got undressed before bed, he would turn his back. She was going to give herself one month before asking for a divorce and returning to her father's house. All their relatives and friends leaned toward believing the bride's family's story that got whispered in ears all around town: that this Azzam boy who didn't like their daughter actually didn't like women at all. They claimed they had proof of it, too. And so Abdelkarim reverted to his original muddled state.

That fleeting marriage left him with nothing but annoying memories of his bedroom having been broken into by a fat, pimple-faced girl who tried daily to cover up those pimples with a layer of pale-colored paint that took an hour to apply. She had appropriated three-quarters of his closet space with her ostentatious dresses and idiotic expensive hats. She would get into a sour mood and suffer for ten entire days with menstrual pains whenever her period came around. She would behave arrogantly toward Hasan al-Owayk, and when he answered her orders with, "As you wish, my daughter," she'd bark at him, "I'm not your daughter!" Abdallah Bey would wink at him to make him feel better. She would snap at Imm Mahmoud if she didn't clean up her bedroom fast enough, sending Imm Mahmoud into the kitchen in tears. She kept criticizing Abdelkarim's attire until he finally surrendered once or twice and put on a brightly colored necktie, which she tied for him. He barely lasted until noon before taking it off, and she would hound him about it, saying, "Have some self-respect! You're an Azzam!"

And she was constantly planning endless dinner parties where she forced him to sit at the head of the table. More than once he would find a million excuses to get up and leave halfway through the evening.

Things settled down after she left, but then a bigger hurricane blew into the city on the heels of the departure of the bride—that reviler of the entire Azzam family, from the grandfather to the father on down, and spreader of every type of disgraceful rumor imaginable. The explosions went off at night at first, making it difficult to predict what places they had reached, and no information came the next day about casualties, since they put life back to normal in the daytime, even if the shops and cafés had locked their doors before the sun had set.

Then the first car bomb went off near the Corniche, hitting a group of morning joggers who'd reached retirement age and liked to go for light runs together. There was a huge dip in electricity after that that drowned the neighborhoods in darkness. People said they would have to wait for a contingent of engineers coming from Austria to fix it. Some unknown masked men came and installed a makeshift checkpoint at the southern entrance to the city and started taking random shots at cars passing by and the people inside them. A second bomb was planted on Monday morning near the statue of Mustapha al-Azzam, which destroyed its base and sent it tumbling to the ground. Going out into the streets had become fraught with danger, and phone calls were nearly extinct while people waited in long lines to buy bread. Abdelkarim spent the time reading and complaining, and erasing the traces of his former wife from his bedroom, while rumors spread saying there was going to be an explosion every Monday morning in order to ruin the week right from the start. The city seemed to have been abandoned by its God. "Emirs" took control of the neighborhoods, each supported by sheikhs who went around the city in armored cars giving fiery speeches and flaunting their weapons. They tried to control people's activities. All their armed men had to do to disperse a crowd or break up a fight was fire some bullets over people's heads. Next came artillery in the public square: 155 mm cannons positioned on top of the nearby hills girded the old neighborhoods. Imm Mahmoud couldn't leave her house anymore and bring them the daily news briefing. The bombing campaign was expanded to reach new territories or to fire rockets haphazardly. Abdallah al-Azzam would venture out onto the porch by himself to listen to the sounds of explosions shattering the night, and Abdelkarim would follow after him sometimes. But one time when he heard his father sobbing loudly, he went back to his room so as not to embarrass him. Sheikh Imad, the emir of the Bab al-Hadid Quarter, who had a good reputation for helping the poor, was assassinated, and in retaliation, ten soldiers were killed at night at the old train station. Schools gave the schoolchildren an open-ended vacation, and news circulated of family and friends leaving for the Gulf or Europe. Some left by sea and headed for Cyprus on trade ships that usually docked in the city's harbor.

Abdelkarim's turn eventually came around. Abdallah al-Azzam's wife talked it over with her daughter in Saudi Arabia, and they agreed that the son-in-law would pay travel expenses for him to go to Paris. He would take up residence there, and study or get a job. The plan was settled the day Abdallah al-Azzam came back gloomy-faced from a meeting of city deputies and dignitaries at the mufti's villa. Hasan al-Owayk buoyed him as he climbed up the steps to the front door, reciting Quranic verses out loud. He sat down, exhausted, in his armchair, and said, in a loud voice with a tone of finality while pounding his staff against the floor, "Abdelkarim! To the airport this minute!"

"*La hawla wa la quwwata illa bil-Laah,*" There is no power and no strength except with God. They took the Bab al-Hadid casualties to the Islamic Hospital. Men, women, children. The hospital director told us about them and asked us out of his intense fear not to tell anyone. He didn't know how many casualties. The medics and ambulance men stopped counting. The morgue was filled to capacity, so they stacked up the bodies out on the sidewalk in plastic bags, and also on the sidewalk across the street. Cars were passing by between them. The smell was unbearable. It even reached the main road, causing the traffic to be rerouted to another street. A crowd of women arrived from Bab Al-Hadid, shouting and chasing behind ambulances from the Red Cross. Some men came, too, to identify their loved ones. The *Mukhabarat* secret service agents who arrived with the first casualties and waited with them asked them their names. They seized their ID cards and then proceeded to take them in a military vehicle for questioning. They pushed the women back, but instead of obeying orders, the women screamed and wailed even louder. So they fired bullets over their heads..."

Abdelkarim's father continued, "The news of these actions spread, and despite calls from the hospital administration, no one dared come to request a fallen son or relative for fear of falling into the hands of the Mukhabarat and ending up in jail with no hope of ever coming back home. The corpses stayed piled up there like that. The hospital director had no idea what he should do with the casualties whose stench was everywhere and had driven people into an indescribable state of unrest. And just now, at the meeting, we decided the only thing to do was to number them and secretly bury them in the Strangers' Cemetery...Get your passport ready. I'll work on getting you a visa. I still have some connections in the French Embassy!"

They waited for things to quiet down, or for a pause in the shelling, and then his father took him in the Jaguar to the airport. Abdelkarim fell asleep in the backseat on the way. His father gave him a long hug and made him promise to pay a visit on his behalf to a beautiful little hotel in the *Quartier Latin* that he had stayed in for three days when he was passing through Paris. The word around town concerning Abdelkarim al-Azzam's absence was that he was pursuing a high-sounding major called "Politics and Economics" at a French university.

Years passed, and things in the city stabilized somewhat without any desire to return ever developing in Abdelkarim's heart. And the news being heard about him was not comforting. It found its way to his cousin Riyad's council sessions by way of some of his compatriots living in the French capital, some of whom said they just happened to bump into him on a rare occasion, and others who lived on the next street over from his residence, which was on the edge of Luxembourg Gardens. They reported he was head over heels in love with someone they called "an actress," a euphemism for a street woman or, as one of them put it with a disdainful gesture, "an emaciated dancer." He says "emaciated" holding his index finger up in the air as an indication of how skinny she was, and insignificant. The witness adds, in front of all the smiling faces present, that he saw her himself walking beside Abdelkarim down a sidewalk on Boulevard de Montparnasse. And even though he didn't stop to greet him and introduce himself, our learned narrator swears that Abdelkarim was spending all his money on her, even if this slanderer took pleasure afterward in telling one of his male cohorts who had been listening, while jealously shaking his head, that she was gorgeous.

Abdelkarim came back from France only one time, to attend the funeral of his father, who died from the infection that had flared up again in his wounded leg after all those years, for reasons the doctors couldn't explain. And so the rumors started up again, this time with a story about Abdallah Bey. According to the story, not long after his marriage, he'd been shot, and then something about getting into trouble with a woman whose sister he had jilted in order to marry another woman. This left the sister in bad shape. She was crying all the time and refusing to eat, until she actually became ill. So her sister hired the person who shot Abdallah Bey. And people said that she was standing in the shadows with the hit man in order to make sure he didn't kill him but only wounded him, so he would have to be reminded his whole life of her sister and remember how he had broken her heart. Abdallah al-Azzam carried that wound his whole life, and then he died from it.

As soon as he got word, Abdelkarim tried to travel back home, but he got caught in the middle of an Air France pilots' strike and ended up getting stuck in Charles De Gaulle airport. He didn't make it home until a full day after his father's burial. Those who knew him well couldn't help but notice a certain liveliness about him and brightness in his eyes that had been missing before he left for Paris. His face seemed more relaxed, his little muscles were toned. He showed interest and was willing to listen, despite being seated there, bereaved, receiving condolences from people who had come directly to him at his house to console him. The evening of his return flight to Paris, he went by himself to the cemetery and stayed there until people at home started worrying about him. Night fell and he still hadn't returned. So Hasan al-Owayk went out after him. He entered the cemetery at night, full of fear, and started calling out for Abdelkarim Bey. He spotted him in the distance sitting down with his head resting on his knees. He shook him by the shoulder to wake him up and then walked him home to his mother who, in addition to being stricken with the grief of losing her husband, had also been made to suffer the deep bitterness of watching his brother and nephew stand there all alone accepting condolences while a few people asked about Abdelkarim, and acted as if his absence from his father's funeral was the kind of behavior they expected from him. His mother was certain she would never have the pleasure of seeing what she'd dreamt of ever come true before she died, she who tried so many times to persuade her husband to make their new house a two-story house.

"We can turn the ground floor into a *reception room*…"

Her parents, who, as she said, were not upper-class people, had a reception room in their house, so why shouldn't the son of Mustapha al-Azzam have a place to receive visitors and supporters?

Abdallah Bey would shoot her a somewhat weary look and then a quick argument would transpire between them:

"Listen, Malakeh, politics is my older brother's concern…"

"Why?"

He'd answer with a tone of exhaustion from having to repeat once again, "That's what my father wanted."

"And what about us? What do we get?"

"Peace of mind."

After a period of languishing in the loneliness of the house that was now emptied of its men, Abdallah al-Azzam's widow decided to go spend some time with her daughter in Saudi Arabia and live with her for a while. She left care of the house to Imm Mahmoud, who had gotten on in years and had a difficult time coming all the way from the American Quarter. So Imm Mahmoud in turn handed over the responsibility to her daughter Intisar, wife of Bilal Muhsin, who could use the income.

"The most gracious people on earth. And the work while they're away is very easy," she told her. "You open the house once a week. Air it out and dust the furniture. Mop the floor and water the flowers out on the patio." Abdallah Bey's wife had decided not to cover the sofas and chairs, and in the beginning she even wanted to leave the refrigerator running, because she didn't know when she might come back. Imm Mahmoud warned Intisar to be very careful and protective of the Azzam family's valuable belongings – carpets and expensive chandeliers and other furnishings. And she did not hold back from warning her that it was absolutely necessary to keep her husband Bilal away from the house and never to let him go with her there. She should even hide the key from him so as not to let him get any ideas about putting his hands on any of their expensive possessions.

3

Bilal Muhsin sought death, but death, it seemed, wasn't interested in Bilal Muhsin. At age twenty-four, he urged his cousin to take him to Bab al-Hadid, during the final blood-spattered chapter that transpired there. He didn't realize, though, that his timing was like the old saying—he was setting out for *hajj* when everyone else was headed back home. The rebels there were in such dire need of men that they accepted anyone who volunteered. Their numbers had dwindled after the Nationalist and Islamic Labor Front dissolved and their allies in the city's eastern suburbs abandoned them. The Front's emir had suddenly spoken out in favor of neutrality. He published a long declaration in which he called for "sparing national blood" and the need to preserve "the Islamic cause." He recalled all the terminology that they had used to stir up the fighting in the first place: the pledge of allegiance, the Arab nation, resistance, and finished it up by saying it was time to disengage from "secondary conflicts." He called the falling of martyrs and the destruction of neighborhoods and the torture of being arrested "secondary conflicts." Then he suggested that others should follow his lead by turning in their weapons to be redistributed to various hiding places. His speech was broadcast on FM radio on a station dedicated to religious programming.

In Bab al-Hadid, Bilal found all the shop doors busted up and chunks of walls and balcony railings strewn all over the streets. There was also a charred Mercedes in front of a branch of the Crédit Populaire bank. Some of the shop owners emptied out their merchandise and abandoned their shops, swearing never to return to that place where, thanks to the fighting, they'd seen their livelihoods go up in flames for the third time.

Bilal was out of work. Every day he heard talk of someone named Abu Khalid who'd blown up a tank at the entrance to the neighborhood, near the traffic circle. People also talked about a group of young men who'd captured an officer and three soldiers they exchanged for the release of some men from Bab al-Hadid who'd been taken prisoner. The names enchanted Bilal, and he developed a desire to be in the company of such heroes, or maybe even join their ranks. They gave him a rifle to carry. He stored it at the Center when he went home each morning. He would spend his days at the American Quarter and then return to the center every evening to report what he'd heard. After his cousin negotiated on his behalf, they also issued him a revolver they allowed him to carry and take home with him for protection. They gave him food rations—rice, sugar, milk, and canned goods—and promised to replenish the rations every month. They also gave him a monthly supply of antibiotics for a sick family member he claimed to have at home, which he sold to the girl who worked at al-Kamal Pharmacy for whatever amount he could get.

Bombings in Bab al-Hadid didn't follow any particular pattern. The important thing was to escape the first strike and take cover in the ground floor of some building. The men kept guard at night, drinking tea at an athletic club they turned into a military headquarters for their local committees. In the middle of the hall there was a ping-pong table and a metal desk with a big black telephone sitting on it that rang non-stop. There was also a fan in the corner that ran twenty-four hours a day. Anyone taking a breather from the task of fighting behind the barricades could saunter over to this place and get the latest news. They listened to radio broadcasts and tried to predict where the next bombs would fall. Fiery nights alternated with calm nights. Bilal wasn't charged with any particular task. Mostly he just lay on the floor, smoking incessantly—they all smoked incessantly—and waited for instructions from Sheikh Imad, the Emir of Bab al-Hadid, who wore a beard but no turban. The sheikh sat behind the desk, letting others answer the phone before passing the receiver to him, beneath a picture of his brother Omar, who died in prison. In the picture, Omar is shaking hands with Yasser Arafat who, at the time the picture was taken, had a big smile on his face that showed his teeth as he looked toward some other person not in the picture. Everyone believed that Omar was taken down by the secret police inside prison. Imad resembled his brother, and behaved like him, too, even dressed like him and wore a similar beard. He divided up and shared "his bread" with them, as they say; always distributed every form of assistance he received equally among his men. He pledged to strike the hand that dared to reach for another person's possessions. He wanted them to walk through the neighborhood with their heads held high, and he emphasized the need for determination; it was the only thing that could tip the balance of the fight. His proof of that was the many calls for solidarity that he received from young men from other quarters requesting his participation in battle, to which he replied that he would not forsake them in their time of need.

Explosions came intermittently. They prayed the dawn prayers and parted ways. Bilal asked about their names, trying to put a face on the heroic deeds he'd heard about. His cousin gave terse answers and advised him not to be too nosy. Bilal smoked a lot and listened a lot. There hadn't been many real confrontations in the battlefield; just some sniping from the opposing barricades, or some shelling that would reach them from the distance. One time they talked in front of him about a plan to sneak up the riverbed and launch an attack on a heavy artillery installation on top of one of the hills overlooking the city. They planned numerous operations they never had the opportunity to carry out.

However, their enemies succeeded in carrying out the biggest operation of all. They lured Sheikh Imad outside the quarter under the pretext of a meeting to plan and discuss his so-called campaign to "Spare National Blood." On his way back from the meeting, a motorcycle stopped in front of his car and two armed men rained bullets down on him and his bodyguard before fleeing the scene. No one dared approach the car. They called out to Sheikh Imad through the window of a nearby building, but got no answer. The car stayed there in the street until the sheikh's supporters from the quarter, who had been waiting for him to come and brief them about the meeting, came looking for him. Bilal was among them. They crossed over to the other side of the river, worried all the while that they might be shot at, at any moment. They finally made their way to him and pulled him out from the car. He wasn't just dead; he was very dead. The men raised him high up on their shoulders. Bilal helped carry him. He had blood stains all over his clothes. They carried Sheikh Imad's bodyguard, too, shouting, "*Allahu Akbar!*" God is Great! and crying in anguish, while the balconies of the nearby buildings filled with shocked onlookers. They carried the two men back to Bab al-Hadid, where they were met by those who'd stayed behind, who rushed to take him down, wash him, and wrap him in a shroud. Two men went back again under cover of darkness to retrieve the car, which was left parked outside Sheikh Imad's house for many years without anyone ever cleaning up the traces of blood and bullets.

They avenged him even before he was buried. Five young men set out with two RPGs and some machine guns, and headed along the northern "irrigation" path. They hesitated over whether or not to let Bilal come with them, due to his lack of battle experience. They were afraid for him and for themselves, worrying that he might get shaken up, drop his weapon, and entangle them in a mess. But he insisted. He got all worked up about it. Believing his feelings were sincere, they decided to take him with them down some paths inside a thick grove of orange trees—the same one that Sheikh Imad had planned to flee through if a quick getaway became necessary; that was after he had heard from "high sources" that they might launch an air attack on Bab al-Hadid. They soon arrived at the abandoned train station, whose Aleppo-Haifa line had stopped running in 1948, the same time the trains stopped going to Beirut and Damascus, as well. Nothing remained of the train station except a stone building, two rusted railroad cars, and some scattered sections of the train tracks. It had been turned into a military post. They could see that the guard was dozing in his chair, with his weapon down at his side. Bilal's heart pounded in his chest. He was scared and ready for death. They told him to secure the back of the road. Two of the young men, whose names would never be disclosed to anyone, knelt down and fired two RPG rockets at the same time, hitting both railroad cars. They knew there would be soldiers sleeping on foam mattresses inside the railcars. They started shouting *"Allahu Akbar!"* and firing their machine guns for cover as they withdrew. It was the first and last time Bilal ever fired a weapon, even if only into the air. They didn't sustain any return fire. As they ran deep inside the orange groves on their way back to Bab al-Hadid, they could hear men moaning and screaming.

The shelling stopped, giving them a chance the next day after the noon prayers to have a funeral for Sheikh Imad. Their great martyr. The entire quarter came out to walk in the procession. For the first time, a group of young men appeared wearing black headscarves with *"La Ilaha Ilallah Muhammad rusool Allah,"* There is no God but God; Mohammad is the Messenger of God, written on them. Some groups from other areas came as well and fired a rainstorm of bullets into the air. The Sheikh's eldest son spoke a few words, wept, and vowed that his father's blood and the blood of his uncle Omar would not have been shed in vain. The groups who had come to Bab al-Hadid departed when they started hearing reports of soldiers killed in their sleep at the old train station. They knew something big was going to happen.

That big thing did happen, after two days of eerie calm during which there was no shelling and only a few random bullets fired here and there. After Sheikh Imad was killed, Bilal didn't leave Bab al-Hadid. He started sleeping at the Center. The nights would pass in a gloomy atmosphere after the number of men taking shifts dwindled. Some of them asked him quietly about the train station operation, and he would just smile without saying anything. The calm was disturbing and the night was heavy until a group of men suddenly barged in on them just before dawn. No one knew how they managed to get past the quarter's checkpoints with such ease. They were wearing tennis shoes and military fatigues. They'd climbed up the stairs without making a sound, and stormed in, pointing their guns at their faces. When one of the men who was keeping watch half-asleep from his chair reached for his rifle, they shot him. He fell to the floor and started moaning in pain. They ordered everyone to sit on the floor and put their hands behind their heads. Their leader was not wearing a face mask, but no one recognized him. People said he was an officer in the Mukhabarat with the rank of colonel. He was holding a list of names and giving out orders. Their guide *was* wearing a mask. He was short and fat and didn't speak so as not to reveal his identity. Most likely he was from Bab al-Hadid. They'd bought him as they'd bought many others. Sheikh Imad always knew who the traitors were, but gave them a chance. He always said that a true son of Bab al-Hadid would never betray them. He didn't want to hurt them, for their parents' sake. The short guide would point to one of the names on the list and then point to one of the men sitting on the floor, and the colonel would put a check mark next to the name. The informant hesitated a little and then whispered something in the colonel's ear, who then called out for Bilal Muhsin to get on his feet and leave the room. The fat masked man followed Bilal out to the entryway. He didn't say a word to him. He looked at him a long time to make sure of the face in the dark, and then, without any warning, punched him hard in the face and then pushed him down the stairs. He pushed him so hard that Bilal crashed against the wall and fell to the ground, maybe to send a message not to look back as he ran away.

Bilal did not follow orders, nor was he able to flee. He fell a second time, and instead of going out into the street, he hid and waited behind a stack of empty medicine and food ration boxes that were piled up near the front door of the building. Sounds of gunfire and explosions came nonstop from every corner of the quarter. A few minutes later, he could hear machine-gun fire up on the first floor, as if it was coming from the cement wall he was leaning against. Some screams and orders ensued, followed by one final, long shower of bullets. One of them emptied the entire clip of his Kalashnikov, pouring its contents into all those bodies as they teetered and gave up their souls, leaving behind utter silence. He didn't hear them leave, only sensed the sound of their footfall as they went down the stairs in their tennis shoes. He pushed the empty boxes out of his way, and instead of standing up on his feet, he propped himself up on all fours and crawled up to the upper floor where the gas lantern was casting light and shadows over the heaps of bodies of the members of the popular front, his comrades, scattered all over the room. One was thrown on top of the ping-pong table; two were sprawled over the metal desk; and the rest were on the floor. He didn't stand up. He just sat there, as if thrown down and killed like the others. Even after the light from the lantern dimmed and finally went out completely, and after the smell of gunfire dissipated and the smell of blood was the only odor filling the room, he just sat there in the dark with his eyes wide open. The sound of gunfire outside stopped and the light of daybreak began to creep in. He could hear the dawn *adhan* call to prayer coming from a distant mosque. At that moment, the fact he was still alive was a heavy, heavy burden.

He slipped between his comrades, weeping silently. He lay down among them until the rising daylight shone on their dead eyes staring at him. He got up, terrified, and began turning their bodies over one by one. He shook them, called out to them in a loud voice, using their names that he loved and their assumed *noms de guerre*. He called out to his cousin, the one who had brought him to them and was now tossed among them on the floor. Then he rushed down the stairs and ran out into the street, gasping *"Allahu Akbar."* He muttered it at first, dozens of times, in order to regain some of his strength, and then he shouted it at the top of his lungs. No one responded and no one shot at him. He heard ululations and screams, but he did not turn to look. The sound of two objects hitting the ground reached him. It sounded more like heavy artillery falling, or at least that's what he imagined in his state of delirium. He did not turn to look. People told him later that whatever they were had been thrown by the men firing on them from the upper floors of the building. Maybe it was because he didn't look right or left that he survived.

The ambulances didn't dare enter Bab al-Hadid before eight o'clock, when they got the green light from the assailants. The emergency workers were wearing gauze masks over their faces as they went around with stretchers. A woman came out from a building and called out to them, letting them know there were dead bodies inside. They worked until noon removing corpses and transporting them to the Islamic Charitable Hospital.

No one seemed to notice Bilal Muhsin's situation. He disappeared from view. The survivors assumed he had died in the massacre, and his name even appeared on a preliminary list of "martyrs" on a flyer that was left on car windshields in the surrounding neighborhoods under the cover of darkness. Then rumors spread that Bilal had left the center around midnight and got out before the attack, despite having been expected to spend the night there since he never usually returned to his own neighborhood before daybreak.

They found ten bodies at the center. Bilal was the only survivor. And since no investigation into a major incident of that type ever ended without the discovery of a collaborator, Bilal Muhsin was the target of everyone's suspicion. He didn't contact anyone, didn't speak to anyone, and didn't tell anyone what happened. They accused him of fleeing, of being afraid, of being an informant. None of the men keeping watch that night was still alive, so there was no one who could corroborate his story. The few young men who managed to get themselves safely out of the organization took shelter in a Palestinian refugee camp in the south, or they managed to board a ship from the Christian port of Jounieh and settled down in Melbourne or Copenhagen.

A young man from Bab al-Hadid ran into Bilal at the Gold Souks. He approached him, shoved him threateningly, and spat on the ground in front of him. Bilal did his best to avoid him. Another man followed him to his neighborhood, cornered him in an alley, and threatened him with a knife to his stomach. Bilal swore by the Quran and the Prophet that he wasn't a traitor and didn't know why the attackers had let him go. He said he was prepared to avenge his Bab al-Hadid brothers in any way they wanted. Bilal didn't convince the man that he was innocent, but the man wasn't certain Bilal was a traitor, either. In the end, he gave him a stern warning and let him go.

He spent years trying to clear himself of blame and trying to find out who it was who had singled him out that night and gotten him out of that room. Every short, fat man he saw reminded him of that man, and heavyset men were few and far between in that area. He stopped on numerous occasions in front of the cobbler at the corner of the street where the Coppersmith Souks were. For a long time, he went after a member of the municipality police. He barged in on him and stared him down until the man threatened to hit him. Bilal sat for long periods trying to remember all his relatives, because he had the feeling that the man who had hit him and pushed him down the stairs had treated him like he was an older brother, rebuking him for getting involved in such dangerous activities. He recalled all his male relatives one by one: his two brothers who were tall and slim like him; his maternal cousins in the village—one who drove a passenger van, and one who drove a tractor.

There was no local man—short or fat—to be found,

and there wasn't any work for him to find, either. He forgot everything he had learned during an entire year of painting cars. He didn't dare go out into the wide new streets where they might recognize him and hunt him down. He wasn't afraid of the people he didn't die with, but the others—the ones who didn't want there to be any witnesses to their murder.

There were occasional acts of retaliation now and then while he tried various jobs that didn't keep food on his table. He sold coffee out of an urn strapped to his back out in the small circle of alleys where he was still safe. And he set up a kiosk where he sold cigarettes on one of the sidewalks, but the municipality shut him down during a short-lived wave of regulations aimed at reclaiming public property. There was a charity center he frequented, and he ended up working there as a porter and a security guard and a delivery man, in return for a small room where he could sleep at night.

He didn't have any friends. He wandered about with his head hanging low, until he bumped into Intisar, the daughter of "Abu Mahmoud" (Husein al-Omar)—Mustapha Beyk al-Azzam's bodyguard. A curious mixture of a mischievous child and an audacious woman, she didn't hesitate to kiss boys older than her or to open her thighs to their playful fingers. After his first rendezvous with her, he spent all his time following her so no one else could have her, because he knew she was easy to get. All this also led him to realize the importance of bathing from time to time, and he even washed his own shirts by hand, until he reached a point where some might even find him handsome. Without much experience, he figured out how to sweet-talk girls and how to get into Intisar's head, causing her to become the one to initiate their intimate meetings.

Eventually, their scandal was exposed when some kids surprised them while they were making out in a dark alley. Word reached Imm Mahmoud, who in turn sent someone to warn Bilal Muhsin that he'd better marry her daughter immediately or be forewarned they would not keep quiet and wouldn't hold anything back. Bilal did not resort to confrontation to defend his pride. In fact, the idea of marriage appealed to him—a woman to keep him company and look after his needs. So, he wrote the marriage contract and married her, despite the absence of her angry mother. They took shelter for a while at the charity center. Bilal couldn't find anyone willing to rent him a room, because everyone knew he was broke and couldn't get decent work. He finally found al-Mashnouq, who made him pay half a year's rent up front. To get the money, Intisar emptied out the savings she'd acquired after taking on her mother's housecleaning work, and saved the situation. They moved into the second floor, and whenever they came in or went out of the house they had to walk through their neighbors' living room on the bottom floor.

Intisar started asking herself early, right after her first son Ismail was born, what on earth had attracted her to Bilal Muhsin—this man she hadn't known anything about except from a few stolen minutes in a dark alley. She deeply regretted having refused other young men, especially after she discovered that Bilal was of little use. In fact, she had to go right back to work the moment she'd figured out what to do with her newborn. The only person she got any help from was al-Mashnouq's wife, who agreed to look after the baby along with her own children whenever Intisar left the house. In the meantime, Bilal resumed letting the whole day drag by, with his grey face and half-shaved beard. His appearance, his clothes, and his miserable countenance were like an extension of the shabby places he stood in for hours on end, watching traffic or the gush of the river's muddy waters that came whenever the snow melted off the high mountains. One thing he didn't hold back on, though, was fathering children. He'd wait until the little one fell asleep in the adjoining room and then he would go to Intisar. He forbade her from kissing him or taking off her clothes, and he pinned her down so she couldn't move. He'd penetrate her just until she began to be aroused and then he would quit the moment he finished satisfying himself. She'd get up to go wash herself and when she got back, he'd be asleep. The only time he got involved with the children was to give them names of people he liked in Bab al-Hadid—the ones he lay beside but didn't die beside. His voice chimed in with the newborn's cries as he shouted in Intisar's face and got so angry he even hit her sometimes. His landlord al-Mashnouq would step in to break up their fights while secretly wishing Bilal would carry out those threats of his which were always accompanied by a solemn oath with right hand raised. Al-Mashnouq was taken by Intisar's back side, especially since it didn't take much time at all after giving birth for her to go back to wearing her tight jeans. The moment he heard her footsteps coming down the stairs, he would go on alert. He relished ogling her long thighs before her face came into view, forcing him to lower his gaze. With his wife getting more and more wrinkled as she sped toward old age, he was more than ready to marry Intisar if Bilal divorced her. The two families would be gathered nicely together in one house whose key he alone possessed and inside which his rules were law and he didn't have to share anything with anyone.

The day Intisar gave birth to her third son, who came prematurely, uprooted and scrawny, due to Bilal's constant violent treatment of her as people said (even though the doctor rejected that theory), her mother, in tears, came running to see her. Imm Mahmoud kept herself under control for years, stubbornly refusing to concede to her miserable only daughter. Then, suddenly, in a single day she let it all go. She barged into al-Mashnouq's house and sped up the stairs without a hello to anyone. She asked Intisar where her husband was, to which Intisar replied that he was out and hadn't been home in days. He had been spending the nights at the charity center, exasperated by the baby's crying. Imm Mahmoud wondered out loud why it was that he only got upset when the babies were born but never when they were being conceived. She wanted to make everything up to Intisar, all those years of estrangement, and so she offered to take Intisar's eldest son Ismail into her care. She would take him to come live with her, from now at age seven until "God knows when." Intisar agreed to it, since he would still be close by. She kissed her mother's hand, who had also made up her mind to bring meals to her daughter twice a week at the very least.

Ismail had never stepped foot in his grandfather's house prior to that. At most he would see it from outside if he ever happened to pass that way. The estrangement between Imm Mahmoud and her daughter had extended to him as well. The house had many spacious rooms and high ceilings, and was furnished beautifully despite some of the wooden window casings having deteriorated and the fact that the walls were in dire need of a new coat of paint. The house's owners had stopped living in it a long time ago. His maternal uncle told him that a famous doctor once lived there and received patients. The rusty metal sign with his name and "Graduate of London Universities" engraved on it was still nailed to the entrance. People with heart disease sought him out. He never used a stethoscope or other examination equipment. He just leaned over and put his ear over the patient's chest—and people said he took his time when listening to women's hearts. That was all it took for him to figure out exactly what was ailing the heart and prescribe the perfect treatment.

Ismail spent many beautiful years living with his grandmother. He went to visit his mother at her house from time to time, too. She'd sit him on her lap, breathe in the smell of him, and cradle him in her arms. Sometimes he would bump into his father on the stairways of the American Quarter. He would find him sitting there cross-legged on one of the steps, smoking cheap cigarettes. Ismail would decline his father's invitation to sit beside him on the ground, but Bilal took solace in having Ismail close enough to touch. He'd give him a bit of whatever he happened to have in his hand—some walnuts or an orange, not knowing where to begin or what to ask him about. He'd look at the boy's trousers, his shoes, and then watch as he descended the stairs and took off running the moment he'd managed to free himself from the snare of that awkward encounter with his father.

Ismail's closest companion was his youngest maternal uncle. Every morning he walked him to the public school where he taught junior-level physics and chemistry. He scrimped and saved every bit of his salary, even depriving himself the pleasure of going to coffee shops, all so he could take one trip every summer to some far-off country other than his own. He traveled to Norway and Vietnam and the Amazon. He'd come back with all sorts of stories and spend the evenings describing places covered in snow year-round and cities filled with skyscrapers. He brought presents for his little nephew, souvenirs and coloring books and boxes of wooden colored pencils. Ismail loved to take his time sitting on the floor, carefully and patiently coloring in houses and birds and girls with ponytails. Those were peaceful days. His grandmother fed him the most delicious meals, and he didn't mix with children his own age. He enjoyed watching the bustle of the city as he peered through the window that overlooked the river and the vibrant Sunday market, and the beautiful Hamidiyya School building whose picture used to be featured on the twenty-five-lira bill a few decades back.

In the afternoon, he liked to stand in front of the window facing the tall buildings whose other sides overlooked the river, and he would hold up a piece of shiny glass to catch the rays of the setting sun. He'd move the glass in various directions until he caused a flash of light to reflect off the glass of one of the buildings' windows. He'd shift it left and right until he sometimes got an answer from some boy or girl holding a similar mirror up on a distant balcony one could barely see with the naked eye. They'd exchange messages with light as though speaking their own private language, while flocks of pigeons crowded the sky against the backdrop of the setting sun and a paper kite hovered aimlessly amid the shouts of vendors and the sounds of old cars beeping their horns along the boulevard.

At night, when the people of the American Quarter were drowning in total darkness due to the lack of electricity, and Ismail grew tired of squinting to read his school books under the flickering candlelight, he would go back to his window and gaze at the Crusader Castle which was lit up from outside by floodlights anchored on telephone poles. Standing there casting shadows off its lofty walls, the only visible thing in the night, the castle seemed much taller than it appeared in the light of day.

Ismail took on the task of bringing lunch to his family at their house, in place of his old and tired grandmother who always tried to avoid her daughter's husband. If ever he bumped into his father, he would give him his portion of the food, which wasn't very much, because Bilal did not eat much. He just smoked and grumbled. As soon as Ismail arrived at the house, he would throw himself into his mother's arms and they would hold each other in a long embrace. Intisar couldn't ever have her fill of hugging him. He would play with his new little brother, and on sunny days, he would agree to a brief outing with his father to the nearby souks. They would drink licorice juice, and then Bilal would walk him over to a corn-on-the-cob vendor. They'd sit on the edge of the "Salty Pool," while Ismail greedily gobbled up his corn before heading back home to his grandma.

But then, one day, Imm Mahmoud died, and the bubble Ismail had been living in suddenly burst.

He and his uncle the schoolteacher had come back from school. They arrived to find her in the large living room, sitting on the rose-colored sofa with the torn upholstery whose stuffing was starting to come out through the holes. Her head was resting on her right arm, her mouth was hanging open, and she was holding a set of prayer beads that she never parted from in recent days. They thought she was asleep, but when they called to her she didn't answer. When her son shook her a little, her head rolled onto her chest. Before sitting down for the last time, she had prepared lunch for them and placed it on the table—a bowl of yogurt and an omelet with chopped parsley.

The pleasure ride that had lasted four years was over. His uncle, who had grown attached to Ismail, offered to take care of him. He could continue what Imm Mahmoud had promised to do. Unfortunately, though, it was the uncle who needed looking after, someone to cook for him and do his laundry. Living all alone that way was not conducive to marriage. And so Ismail returned to al-Mashnouq's house. He couldn't find a place for himself in his parents' two rooms except a spot to sleep in at night somewhere on the two mattresses that lined the bedroom floor, which the three brothers shared. Sometimes, without warning, the little one would wet the bed at night, just before dawn, and his brothers would get soaked. The next night they'd sleep without the sheets that reeked of urine. Life was difficult. Intisar was pregnant once again and wasn't doing housecleaning work because the entire

Azzam family was abroad. Her legs were swollen and her face was splotched. She swore this would be the last pregnancy. As for Bilal, he went back to his usual activities, sitting in front of the TV with al-Mashnouq for a little while without saying a word, before heading outside to roam about.

Likewise, Ismail was forced out into the quarter's stairways and alleyways. He ended up joining the "Sons of the American Quarter" gang. He passed all the tests: flexing biceps, lighting up cigarette butts he picked up off the ground, and hitting on girls. He proved himself rather quickly with an incident the boys his age spread around with much admiration. He had been walking down the street with his handicapped brother, having a nice stroll, passing by the shop windows as his brother liked to do. Ismail was very patient with him. He answered his naive questions and bought him raspberry-flavored ice cream if he had the money. Suddenly he noticed there was someone following them. Two kids who didn't pass them, just kept stopping whenever Ismail and his brother stopped. Ismail turned around to take a quick peek at them and saw they were imitating his brother's awkward limp and trying to hold back laughing at their own performance.

"Stay here," Ismail warned his brother. "Don't move. I'll be right back."

He grabbed one of the boys, threw him to the ground, and when he didn't find anything to hit him with, butted him with his head. His brother cheered him on as best he could. Some onlookers gathered around and tried to separate Ismail from his adversary who appeared to be in total shock, with blood dripping down his forehead, but managed to yell, "I'm going to report you to the police!"

To this Ismail retorted, "Tell your friend I'm coming after him, too!"

Ismail's uncle oversaw his studies. He reviewed all his lessons with him and helped him to finish his *brevet* diploma before drowning in his addiction to alcohol. All alone in that big house, he dreamt of the countries he'd visited and the women he didn't conquer on his travels. He detested the people in his neighborhood and saw himself as a prisoner inside that "shabby" quarter. He grew crankier with the passing of each new day. He yelled at his pupils and even hit them sometimes. He started taking tranquilizers without a prescription. He was plagued with misgivings day and night, without anyone to listen to him. He got hold of a recording of the speech by Gamal Abdel Nasser in June of 1967, after his army's defeat in the Six-Day War, in which he announced his resignation as president of Egypt. He waited for the commemoration of that resignation day to come around, and as soon as he arrived home from school, he started drinking whiskey while listening to the recording of the resignation speech, the volume turned up full blast. He played it over and over again, while weeping and sobbing, into the middle of the night.

Ismail enrolled in a vocational training institute, mechanical section. During the first days, he was happy there, wearing the blue overalls he wasn't allowed to take home. But he couldn't stand all the homework and the gloomy teachers wearing frowns on their faces all the time, and so he started skipping a lot. He would head toward the institute in the morning, but before arriving he would suddenly stop, turn around, and go back the way he came. He felt the entire day should belong to him. He would pass by his uncle Mahmoud's shop, who wouldn't even bother himself to say hello, and then continue on to wait for his uncle the teacher to come outside the school during the ten o'clock break. Tired, stumbling, and hands trembling, his uncle would come out to buy cigarettes, and he'd give Ismail some money, too. But it wasn't long before his uncle ended up in the government hospital after a drunken fall in which he sustained a broken shoulder and nearly gouged his eye out. And so Ismail's school money dried up, as did his spending money, since his uncle was no longer convinced, amid his weighty thoughts, of the necessity of learning, an idea he had returned with from his last trip to "the land of the Incas" as he called it.

When Intisar asked Ismail about school, he fed her lies he'd concocted ahead of time. And then, one day, he decided to shave the sides of his head and leave a patch down the middle which he dyed blue and red. His little brother pouted for days, wanting to imitate him, and when he finally gave up on the idea, to spite him he tattled to his mother that his brother had also gotten a tattoo on his back. Intisar waited until Ismail was asleep and lifted his shirt to see if it was true. When she did, she found a frightening drawing on his back of a winged creature with a gaping mouth and sharp fangs and talons. She woke him up only to hear him casually tell her it was the angel of death.

With the birth of her newest baby girl, the house filled with the sounds of her crying day and night. Al-Mashnouq's wife would rush to her with some sugar water to help quiet her down. She'd sleep two hours and cry the remaining hours of the day as if her insides were being stabbed with a knife. Intisar swore that from that day forward she would not let Bilal near her. She was done with him, done with the stench of him, too. The next time he decided to sleep at home, she was going to place the baby between them and put an end to it right away.

Meanwhile, on clear days, Ismail spent the nights with his gang on one of the stairways, sitting just like his father used to, with his arms wrapped around his knees. He and his buddies cursed and plotted all sorts of mischief. On Sunday mornings, they waited for the Christian women to come for liturgy at the Church of the Virgin, which, with its locked doors, was perched at the highest point in the American Quarter. They watched them as they flocked in wearing scarves on their heads that didn't look like the hijabs their own mothers wore. They passed by, accompanied by a young priest. While he said mass, the Muslim kids spied on them through the keyhole in the door and winked at each other, especially at the moment when the incense filled the air and the priest chanted Syriac hymns, before raising his chalice, signaling it was time for the women to line up to take communion.

Sometimes Ismail and his buddies would pounce on the old sheikh who lived in the quarter who specialized, as his sign indicated, in curing "Hemorrhoids, Eczema, Scabies, Leprosy, 'Electricity in the Head,' Epilepsy, Ringworm, Cancer, and All Other Ailments, with the help of God." One of Ismail's adolescent buddies who had gone to see the sheikh at one time with his cross-eyed brother, told them that he knew the drawer where the sheikh kept his money. They all entered his hole of a clinic together, making a lot of noise. He had fallen asleep in his chair, but when he heard their footsteps and voices, he straightened up and started reading from the Quran that was always open there on the table in front of him. They surrounded him from all sides as Ismail approached him complaining of aching testicles. The sheikh told him to pull down his pants and his underwear. When the sheikh bent down and started rubbing some black ointment on Ismail's crotch, his buddies started winking and snickering at each other: that was their chance to rob the money from his drawer. They used some of it to pay the doctor for his troubles. Ismail, who had black ointment smeared all over him, insisted that he deserved a larger cut than the others, considering what he'd had to go through. So, they gave him a double share and divided the rest among themselves, before disappearing. No one saw them in the quarter for days. They stayed away from the area and headed to the city suburbs, over near the old grist mill where the water was deep and the rushes were high. They dove in, naked, and came out of the water stinking of the sewage that poured into the river from all the neighborhoods up on the surrounding hills.

To earn a tiny income, Ismail volunteered to stand at traffic intersections and wait for people to roll down their car windows so he could hand them colorful flyers advertising restaurants or clothing stores. Then one day, a big fancy car pulled up next to him, driven by a lady wearing dark sunglasses that covered half her face. When he leaned in, she stroked his cheek and handed him a hundred thousand lira note before driving away. He used the money to get himself a membership at an athletic club located at the entrance to the Tailors' Souks, where he spent his time lifting weights and building his muscles. He spent the rest of the money on renting a motor scooter that he rode through the city streets all the way to the port, where he stopped to gaze at the ships sailing out to sea.

Parliamentary elections were approaching, and all the way down the hill the fronts of all the buildings in the quarter that overlooked the city were plastered with posters of politicians. Anyone walking or driving by in a car below could see them posted along the cluttered route. Campaign managers would pay a building owner fifty dollars to allow them to put up a wooden billboard with a giant picture of their smiling candidate on it, along with pithy slogans like, "Of the People and For the People," or "An Icon of Loyalty." For that price, the building's inhabitants happily agreed to spend two months living in the dark. This particular year, the number of these billboards doubled when a nouveau riche entered the race. Rumor had it he'd amassed his formidable fortune selling portable telephones. His slogan was "The Real Thing." He offered building owners a hundred dollars and a case of foodstuffs for each poster they let him put up, and so the American Quarter got transformed into an endless, multicolored display. At the same time, a young sheikh newly returned from Pakistan had been roaming around the quarter's alleys and climbing its endless stairways agitating. Some of the time he preached against the portrayal of anything connected to the human soul in pictures as sacrilege, as it was akin to Divine Creation, and other times he condemned it as buying votes and called for a boycott of the elections, because to vote would go against the precepts of an Islamic state. Some young people listened to him. Ismail got fired up and organized a campaign of his own at night. Before sunup the next day, he'd managed to tear down or deface most of the posters, and the ones that were hard to reach he splattered with paint from a distance, smearing the new candidate's mouth and eyeglasses. In turn, the campaign manager rushed to send someone to take the posters down, since the pictures were so distorted they no longer resembled the candidate.

A few days later, some police officers came knocking at the door when the name Ismail Muhsin cropped up on the police interrogation list. They left a message for him to come down to the station. The First Lieutenant just wanted to ask him a few questions. But Intisar got scared, and the only place she could think to hide Ismail was at the Azzam house, now that Abdelkarim had come back from Paris and taken up residence there once again. After that, Ismail gained a certain level of notoriety in the American Quarter, and other activities he had nothing to do with also got attributed to him.

News of his deeds reached Yasin al-Shami who sought him out and offered him a job "helping him" in his bakery.

Yasin sold *mana'eesh* and *lahm bajeen,* pizza-like snacks and meat pies, in his little shop, and customers stood at a long marble counter eating from cheap plastic plates filled with creamy strained *labneh* yogurt with olive oil and small loaves of fresh hot bread. His hungry customers devoured their food facing the wall, with nothing in front of them but a colorful list, in alphabetical order, of the Companions of the Prophet and their good deeds—from Ja'far al-Tayyar to Abdullah Ibn Abbas, nicknamed "the Sea," to Uthman Ibn Talha to whom the Prophet gave the key to the Kaaba the day of the Conquest of Mecca. While Yasin turned toward the oven to adjust the flame and slide out the baked pastries with his long wooden paddle, he would ask Ismail to keep his eyes peeled in the opposite direction, toward the customers, while the two of them stood with their backs against each other. He warned Ismail never to touch money with his own hands, but to wait for him to open the cash register, inside which Ismail noticed on the very first day the presence of a green hand grenade, which Yasin would pick up and replace in the back of the drawer whenever it rolled to the front. Yasin was a nice guy. He paid Ismail weekly, as was the custom in Melbourne where he'd been exiled for several years. And whenever he spotted Ismail's little brothers who might happen to pop their heads inside the bakery to smile and say hello, al-Shami would insist that Ismail send out to them fresh *mana'eesh* with cheese and loaves of bread hot out of the oven. They would make a small opening in one and watch the steam rise up; they were delicious to eat just plain.

After several months of standing with his back to the oven, the son of Bilal Muhsin began showing signs of that characteristic stiffness that often appears in young men who, upon nearing the age of twenty, suddenly find the right path. And this in the same boy who used to climb to the very top of the quarter and ski down the steps, from top to bottom, on two wooden planks, risking breaking all his bones at the slightest skid. Now he walked all alone, with his head hanging low, not hurrying his steps. One after another, his neighborhood buddies started keeping their distance from him. It was as if he'd suddenly grown old. If he ever spoke to them now, it was to discourage them from doing this or that type of thing which, not so long ago, he did with them. At first they thought he was playing a joke on them, but eventually they just ignored him while he prayed, fervently, five times every day and got up at dawn to perform ablutions and kneel in prayer—something that made his younger brother laugh to see him do through half-opened eyes. He postponed letting his beard grow, as per the advice of his sheikh who recommended waiting for it to get thicker first. And he also promised to get himself proper religious clothing.

Intisar didn't admit to herself that her son had "changed" until she heard it from her neighbor, al-Mashnouq's wife.

"He's *matured*," she told her, and mentioned that whenever he passed by them in the entryway, he made a point to say, "*As-salaamu 'alykum*," without looking in the women's direction. Intisar was very pleased with him when she discovered he kept a copy of the Quran under his pillow. Likewise, her heart filled with joy the first time she saw him coming out of the Attar Mosque amid a crowd of men just after Friday prayers. At the time, she slowed her steps, savoring the sight of him as long as she could. Then he started refusing to shake hands with women, and he bought her a conservative religious robe to wear. He tossed it onto the bed saying that women must not wear tight clothes. Then one day he did something she never imagined he would do. He made his bed himself, carefully folded his pajamas, brushed his teeth with toothpaste and a toothbrush, performed the morning prayers, and left. She started noticing in him the things her neighbor had described. She saw something in his eyes, a slanted look, a desire to escape. He avoided making eye contact with her. She would call him by his name when speaking to him and deliberately doted on him, called him "*habibi*." This made him furious. He would bark terse answers at her from wherever he was, without even turning in her direction. For the first time in his life, he'd started saving up money from his job, enough to support them. He'd slip some money into his father's pants pockets while he was asleep, and he provided for his handicapped brother. A little later, she noticed how his voice had changed, had become thick and heavy, as if it were emanating from some new place within him. He eradicated laughing and joking from his demeanor; he was always calm and collected. He bore his buddies' sarcasm with patience, bore everything with patience. When his mother came home from the Azzam house in the evening, she would find him sitting quietly in his room, all alone, thinking and gazing at the blank white wall in front of him.

It took months for his transformation to unfold at the bakery, but he carried out his coup at home in one single day.

That morning, as was her habit whenever she knew she wouldn't be home in time to greet the children when they returned in the afternoon, she gave Bilal a to-do list.

"Buy some eggs and string cheese with black seeds. I have to stay late at the Azzam house today," she said, measuring her words and her tone very carefully as she faced him, trying to avoid making him angry.

"And get some bread and some olives, too," she added. Then she repeated the list so he wouldn't forget anything, "Eggs, cheese, bread, and olives," and hurried down the stairs. She disappeared before she could have the chance to see the look of displeasure in his eyes as he brought his hands to his cheeks in dismay.

On her way home, though, she worried he'd forgotten to get the things she asked for, so she made her way to the bakery and to the grocery store and bought everything. She came into the house carrying the shopping bags. She wasn't expecting her husband to be home at that time. When he saw her, he had a fit.

"You thought I'd let the children go hungry, didn't you?"

"And that's exactly what you did!" she replied, perhaps a bit too hastily.

Every single God-given day, he did something to make her reveal his inadequacy. He never tried to prove his perpetual bankruptcy to her by pulling out his empty, shabby pockets. He never said anything or made up excuses. All he ever did was scream in her face and raise his hand to her. She was the one who helped him maintain a bit of his manhood, even if by deceit. She would ask him to fix the stove, for example, complaining of the constant smell of gas in the kitchen, and he wouldn't do it. So, she would get someone to secretly come and fix it, without telling him, to make it seem like he'd been the one to fix it. She put up with his shouting, bore it when he pushed her or hit her on the shoulder.

He was about to hit her when Ismail suddenly appeared. His eyes glimmered as he grabbed his father's wrist. By coincidence, Ismail had gotten home just behind his mother, but he had lingered on the steps when he heard his father's screaming. He waited, hoping the squabble would end, but when he realized his father had reached the limit of his shouting and cursing and was about to turn violent, he couldn't contain himself.

Bilal tried to free himself, but Ismail's grip was very strong.

"You will not hit her!" he screamed.

His warning applied to the future, too, which he indicated with his hands and with his voice.

No one could have foreseen Ismail's turning out this way—determined and iron-willed, and looking directly into his father's eyes. Bilal relaxed his muscles, and Ismail loosened his grip.

He had clashed with him one other time before that, when Bilal had gone after the cheap bottle of whiskey he kept hidden in the kitchen and didn't find it. Ismail acknowledged having thrown it away and insisted he would not allow alcohol to enter the house, threatening his father with the burning fires of hell and listing off all his sinful behavior in a loud voice: "You don't pray, you don't fast, and you drink, too?"

Bilal didn't sleep at home that night. He wandered here and there. His anger subsided and was replaced by a deep feeling of satisfaction, a kind of happiness he couldn't explain. He eventually ended up at his usual secret refuge, the foam mattress at the charity center. He slept very well and waited until the next morning before going back home. He waited outside, sitting on the steps. When one of al-Mashnouq's children came out, he asked him to call Ismail for him.

Ismail soon appeared at the door, with a stern look on his face, prepared to confront his father again.

"Come," Bilal said as he stood up and started back down the stairs.

His father appeared determined. He would not be denied. "Where to?"

"Follow me," he repeated in a serious tone.

They walked through the souks, the son following the father, prodded by the mystery of it all. When they reached the traffic circle, he asked once again, "Where are we going?"

Again, no answer. Instead he took him by the hand as they rushed across the busy street. From there, the view extended all the way to the sea—a vast, bare landscape strewn with all sorts of debris, and dotted with little hills of white dirt. Bilal signaled to a truck driver he knew and so he stopped, and the two of them climbed into the back of the pickup and sat with their legs dangling out the back. Ismail yielded to his father, possibly to make up for their fight the night before. They got out near the train station. Bilal stopped around a hundred meters away.

"Here!" he said. Ismail stared at him in disbelief after having given up trying to get some information out of him. He let him finish his little show. Bilal turned around and pointed into the distance.

"We came on foot, at night. From over there. There was no moon and no light to reveal us. And this whole area was all orange groves. The guys knew their way around them by heart."

Bilal looked around in all directions, as if suddenly noticing the situation for the first time. "There isn't a single tree left!" he said in surprise.

He went back to the spot he had been pointing to, next to the remnants of one of the orchard walls.

"We crouched here, took aim, counted one, two, three, and fired two RPG missiles simultaneously. There was one big explosion as we shouted, 'Take that from Sheikh Imad!' 'And from Omar,' one of the guys said as we stood up to make our exit. They went up in the hellfire. We saw two of them jump out of a railcar, their bodies engulfed in flames."

"You know how to fire an RPG?" Ismail asked.

Bilal didn't look up or answer him. His face was turned to hide his tears. Ismail left him alone and walked over to the train station. He stopped near the black railcar. Bilal got hold of himself when Ismail came back beside him.

"We finished them off with our machine guns and turned back in the dark of night," he said quickly, not wanting to drag out the telling of his heroic deeds. Then he asked his son not to tell anyone.

"Especially not your mother!"

He knew Intisar was his weak spot.

On the way back, Ismail was also satisfied, knowing in his heart that his father was not a coward, was not totally useless. He did not have to be ashamed of him. But he hesitated over making a final judgement and planned to ask the advice of his sheikh. Bilal was also silent. His actions against those who had killed Sheikh Imad spoke louder than words. It was only when they reached the bottom of the stairways up to the quarter that he put his hand on Ismail's shoulder and whispered, "There's a gun hidden in the house. It's yours now. Look after yourself and your brothers."

"Where is it?" Ismail asked.

"Under the mattress, on my side of the bed...It only has one clip in it."

They bid each other goodbye as if they would not see each other again for a very long time. With that, Bilal felt a heavy burden lifted from his shoulders. Intisar now had Ismail all to herself, after having shared him with her mother for many years. Now Bilal could disappear from the house, sleep out, and run away without having to worry. With Abdallah Bey Azzam's son having moved back into his family's house, Intisar would be able to make enough money to keep the children fed and clothed without a problem.

4

The first time Abdelkarim al-Azzam saw Valeria Dombrovska was in Paris, on the Route 21 bus, in the middle of rush hour.

She was draped in a black trench coat that was unfastened except at the neck, where it was tied with a ribbon. The coat was large enough to fit two women her size inside it. She sat down on the seat beside him and traced a square on the foggy window with her finger. She reached into her purse for a scarf and wrapped it around her neck. When she stood up to get off the bus, her little leather wallet got left behind on the seat. Abdelkarim picked it up and followed after her. She thanked him, in a strange accent, and he invited her to the nearby café. She sat down without taking off her coat. He quickly discovered that his French was better than hers. She ordered only water and could tell that he was new to Paris. She left a few minutes later, but on her way out, she left an envelope on the table with a card inside it and told him that this time he didn't have to give it back to her; it was his to keep.

She'd left him a "special" invitation to see the *Nutcracker* at the Opéra Bastille, and along with it, those big blue eyes of hers that seemed to say he was the one man in the world she'd always been waiting for; he was her amazing discovery with words that dazzled her even before they rolled off his tongue. Then, suddenly, she walked away, pulling the hood of the trench coat over her head as she crossed the street under a light rain. Without looking back, she disappeared down the crowded sidewalk.

A few days later, he went to see the ballet. He hadn't realized that throughout the performance she had been dancing right in front of him the whole time. It wasn't until the end, when she took center stage with a group of dancers to take a bow, that he recognized her. His heart started pounding when her big eyes spotted him sitting there in one of the first few rows.

He stopped in front of the nearby flower shop, perplexed, until the owner stepped in to help. "Who would you like to send flowers to?"

"A dancer…a ballerina."

"Then white irises, of course."

Her shop was next door to the opera house and she was used to catering to admirers. She pulled out a flower and waved it in front of him, bending the stem between her fingers to draw attention to the supple flower head.

He looked over the ballet program he was holding, wrote down her name, shut his eyes and wrote, "I'm stunned!" He signed it, "Passenger from the Route 21 bus, Luxembourg Station."

Out of modesty, he decided not to include his phone number. He stood for several seconds at the red light, his arms wrapped around the bouquet of irises. But when the light turned green, he didn't cross the street. Suddenly, he imagined himself standing before her— assuming he could get to her in her little dressing room backstage where she would be changing out of her costume and removing makeup from her face—tongue-tied, not knowing what to say. His story with her could lose all its luster and magic because of one inadequate move. And so, he decided to go back to the flower shop and have the flowers delivered to her instead. He headed back home, on foot, into a pleasant though chilly Paris night, where he didn't know a soul. He whistled a tune as he walked, enjoying every step in his comfortable new shoes, passing a tall man walking his little dog that was dressed in a blue sweater, and two female soldiers who were walking briskly side-by-side, whispering and then erupting in laughter.

He drank too much red wine, and went to sleep.

The next morning, he was jolted awake by a tumult of emotions. A wave of nostalgia came over him like an ocean wave hitting the sandy seashore, rendering it shiny and fragile. He stayed in his apartment, keeping to himself, mesmerized by the image of the "Nutcracker" ballerina swaying beneath the Paris rain in her trench coat, or as a stark white vision standing before the audience to take a bow. In his mind, these images mingled with that of beautiful Ophelia in her blue velvet dress, floating like a big lily on the surface of the water.

Then for a while, settling into life in Paris occupied his time. He made his way to the Saudi Contracting Company, where he was supposedly employed as an assistant to the manager. It was an easy job to do in return for the monthly wage he received. Plus, he never got in trouble for being absent from work. He also went to the Paris prefecture to renew his residency visa. They sent him to the top floor, Office 36, where a handsome young man, possibly younger than himself, wearing a floral bow tie greeted him with a handshake. The young man opened the conversation by telling Abdelkarim he knew a lot about the "big" family he belonged to. He knew that his grandfather had led demonstrations and protests against the French mandate, but he also knew that now things had changed. He gave him back his papers and assured him he would be granted a ten-year stay.

He frequented the dark cinema houses, those places he hadn't been allowed to enter as a child. He sparked up some fleeting friendships, but then he would see her again, looking down at him from the billboard at a bus stop, taking a dance step on tiptoes with two other ballerinas, behind the star of Don Quixote. On the same day, white Ophelia would also look down at him with eyes wide open, from posters at the metro station, on newspaper kiosks, in the pages of the Paris cinema and theatre guidebook.

And so, the hunt for her was on.

Valeria. Place of birth: Belgrade. Artistic career: over at age forty. He did everything he possibly could in a city like Paris: sent her another bouquet of white irises, again not daring to deliver them in person. He wrote only one phrase on the card: *Your eyes*, and no signature. He would forget her only to have her creep back into his thoughts once again. During this quest of his, he completely fell apart. He went out with lots of women, not really knowing where things might end up with them. Every time he saw her looking down at him from behind the sad knight, he would resume his search for her, until he finally stumbled into her. On a random street corner, they crossed paths and met face-to-face.

"You?" she exclaimed with delight.

They dashed to the nearest café. He didn't know where to begin. They sat in silence for a few minutes while his shock subsided, and then he started talking, discussing the differences between various schools of ballet and between the opera, the operetta, and the opera bouffe. She smiled, not taking her eyes off him, reading what he was saying with his facial gestures more than his words. He seemed real and spontaneous. Once he let himself speak naturally, his nervous facial tics disappeared.

He got everything off his chest.

"I had a red marker and on every poster I could reach I would draw a big red circle around your crowned head. I sat forever in the café across from the center where I assumed your ballet troupe would be rehearsing, but to no avail. Then I contacted a friend of mine in the French police department. He was a bit surprised by my request, but he gave me the address they had for you on file. That's how I found out you live in this area. So, I made it a habit every day to pass this way, down the street where you live, on my way out or my way back home, whether to work or to go shopping. I did that every day until I finally ran into you, which, statistically, was bound to happen eventually. And maybe it took a little too long, because after a while I'd started to forget the reason I was doing it in the first place."

"And here I am!"

He finished his grand confession by taking a little bow before his audience that was a lot like the bows she often took on stage at the end of a show. She didn't even ask his name. She just took him by the hand, and in total silence, they headed off together towards the bank of the Seine. Standing there on the Alexander III bridge, she alternated her gaze between his face and the surface of the water.

"Where on earth did you come from today? You are my birthday present."

And so, he became her shadow.

She'd go from her apartment out to the street and find him there at the entrance to her building waiting for her. He accompanied her to the theatre, went to all her performances, and when she came out from the performers' entry door after the dance troupe had parted for the evening, she would find him standing there, calmly. She would smile shyly to the other ballerinas and he would take her home. They would walk together a short way, but end up taking a taxi because she was tired. She would kiss him on his cheeks and then they would part ways. The next day she would ask him, "Aren't you going to get tired of me?"

He reminded her of her appointments, picked out her clothes for her, carried her groceries, until finally one day she asked him up to her apartment. A large studio with a huge window giving way to a flood of daylight. A big bed—too big for such a tiny ballerina. Pillows tossed to the floor, a television, books, and pink-and-white ballet shoes all over the place. And four miniature trees set on a shelf near a window getting direct sunlight.

"I have a tiny life as you can see," she said as she brought him some tea. "I take good care of my feet and my little bonsai trees. That's about it."

He knew about feet. Men's feet and women's feet. Egyptian ones and Greek ones. Twenty-eight bones, more than a hundred tendons, and twenty muscles. They get inflamed, they swell, the toenails become ingrown. Dancers go up on their toes and the bones crack. Sometimes the sharp pains flare up right in the middle of a dance solo. She puts her feet up on the sofa and Abdelkarim, sitting beside her, holds them in his lap like a treasure, massages the toes, rubs ointment on them, spreads them apart, and very carefully binds each toe with bandages to give her some relief. She hugs him and begs him to stay, and so they spend the night. Neither one gets a moment of shut-eye as they drown each other in a never-ending frenzy of passionate kisses. Then she curls up in a little ball in his lap and sleeps with the rising dawn.

In the morning, he goes back willingly to his office, where he takes interest in some businessmen from his country taking a vacation in the French capital. They shop for fancy clothes and jewelry during the day and plan some type of entertainment at night. He makes a few phone calls, cancels appointments, says some nice things to the French secretary, and hurries home to take his ballerina to dance practice. She managed to get him permission to enter the huge mirror-lined studio. That's where he became acquainted with Bertrand the photographer. For the whole hour, Bertrand silently watched the practice sessions with utmost attentiveness, observing every move. And then he would stand up all of a sudden and start nodding, squatting, backing away, coming close, following them to the backstage area while taking a rain shower of photos. They were used to him being there and didn't react to him in the slightest while he snapped shots of their every step and every rest, their chatter, their laughter, and their concealed pain. Abdelkarim went with Bertrand to his photography studio. They had become friends. He had pictures of dancers all over the place and prints by Toulouse-Lautrec and Edgar Degas. Bertrand said that he was trying to do with photographs what the two artists had done with oils and pastels. Back light, silhouettes, roses unfolding, fragile bodies, dark corners of fatigue. He took shots of them as a group, clustered together. Arms, legs, and light, focusing on shoulders or hair, colorful transparent tulle, bright hair ribbons. A flower unfolding. He gave Abdelkarim an enlarged black-and-white photograph of Valeria.

Valeria…who Abdelkarim knew had cured him. Thanks to her, he had been delivered from the bouts that had troubled him for years, and he forgot his dark voids. He stabilized, floated on the surface of the passing days. He slept well. When his sister came to visit him in Paris with her two small children, she said his face was "lit up." He took them to Euro Disney and gave the children shoulder rides down Champs-Élysées Boulevard as they shouted with glee. He became very effective at his job. He set his priorities, improved marketing strategies, and optimized buying and selling processes. And each day he would hurry home to her. The only time he worried was when she talked at length on the phone in her native Serbian, in a different tone—the kind used for worrisome family matters, obscure problems that were out of his reach. Her voice would change completely, and her whole agile body would cringe before she hung up the phone and walked over to him. She would send forced smiles his way to hide the anger that bubbled up whenever she saw the incoming call was coming from "Mom" or "Belgrade." They would start kissing again, the one gazing into the eyes of the other, and declare their everlasting love while constantly fearing goodbye.

"If I were to lose you, who could I call?"

"And if *I* were to lose *you*?"

She never asked him about his family, but the day he came back from his father's funeral, he read to her what he had written in the margins of a newspaper while sitting impatiently on the flight back to Paris: "*My father is the house's bridge, an olive tree that shades us, unbroken by the wind; my mother is an elder tree, and I will always be the fragile orange tree.*" She rushed to him and hugged him a long time. Then she looked into his eyes, hesitating before asking, "Are you going to give me an orange bonsai tree?"

He spent a whole week searching everywhere, but only got the sort of answers that said orange bonsai trees are very rare or that it's very difficult to grow orange trees in containers. Finally, he came across a miniature tree with "Bitter Orange" on its tag. It was a skinny little tree with three small green fruits. It leaned to one side like a young woman with a long neck letting her wet hair fall freely to one side to comb it. He brought it to her, filled with joy. Then he started helping her with practice. They pushed the furniture against the walls, clearing some open space in the center of the room. He held her waist as she spun around doing pirouettes on the tips of her toes. He lifted her up and tossed her down so she could practice landing on her tired feet. Then he would stand beside her and raise her leg as high as possible. They would stand like that for several minutes.

She gave him a key to her apartment. He would let himself in when she wasn't there and tidy up. He'd take her worn-out pink-and-white slippers home to his own apartment. He also had piles of colorful little leotards, and it may well have been during that period that he developed that dancer's gait one might notice about him today.

One sunny morning, he went up to the fourth floor where her apartment was, rang the doorbell, and got no answer, so he used his key to enter. Taped to the window, he found a letter from her.

I must be crazy like my mother. She enrolled me in the Belgrade Classical Dance Institute when I was five years old, under the tutelage of a sadistic instructor. This she did to make me into what she had been incapable of making me herself. Then she left my father with no warning and took off with a circus man. My father shut himself off inside the house, languishing in grief, despite my brother's and my efforts to lift his spirits. I discovered a few days ago that I am pregnant, but I didn't tell you. I immediately decided to keep the baby. My life here in Paris is over. There is no room for pregnant women or mothers in the world of dance. I don't know why I chose you, to break your heart and my own, and leave. Don't look for me. Don't follow me. I know you are capable of that. And don't ask your friend the policeman, because he won't be able to find me this time. I've left his country. I will go on dancing alone for my own sake, in my room or on a balcony overlooking the Danube where it joins

*the Sava. Take what you want of my things. Look after
my little trees. I took only the orange tree with me, to
remind me of you every day...*

*P.S. I didn't tell the landlord I was leaving. He'll find
out for himself.*

He wouldn't believe it, couldn't accept it. Surely, she would
come back. She was joking. She was testing him. She'd hardly
taken anything with her. Just a few of her clothes and some
CDs. All her books were still standing on the shelves. She
hadn't shown any signs, only the family problems on the phone.
He wouldn't give in. He continued coming to the apartment—
locked himself in, remembered some of the dance steps, tried
to imitate his ballerina. Then he'd water the little trees and
wait for her. He waited for the phone to ring, and whenever
it did, he trembled with excitement. But usually it was just
one of the other ballerinas from the dance studio calling to
find out if she was alright, since she'd missed practice. Or
maybe the theatre administration had noticed her absence. Or
a bank employee was calling to offer her some new service.
She just left everything as it was and walked away. She had
to come back. Then a woman from Belgrade called. When he
first heard the voice, he thought it was her. His blood started
coursing through his veins. But then it became clear that the
speaker didn't know French. Still he thought it must be her
playing a joke on him. But in the end, he was forced to say
himself using a few simple phrases in English, "Valeria isn't
here." He was polite, though, and guessed she was her sister.
He continued paying the rent for her. That was something she
had entrusted him with a long time ago, along with numerous
other little daily tasks he did for her.

He started missing a lot of work at the Saudi company where he was employed. He went on following his girlfriend's routine as if she were still out there somewhere, spying on him, testing to see just how attached he was to her. She could reappear any moment. He got his pajamas and his booze and moved into her apartment. He listened to all the CDs she left behind and gazed at what clothes and socks and shoes she'd left in her closet. He tried to replace her with her things. He was determined to resist, to ward off reality, until his own body betrayed him. He slept overnight at her apartment and in the morning, he couldn't get up. He was consumed by an unending desire to sleep. When he finally managed to sit up on the edge of the bed, his hands were numb and his lips wouldn't stop trembling. He battled it on his own for twenty-four hours. He didn't call anyone. He dragged himself to the bathroom, made himself drink some water. The next night he was overcome with uncontrollable vomiting, and so he called an ambulance and got admitted to the hospital.

This happened to coincide with his brother-in-law's visit to Paris to sign a construction contract for a luxury hotel in Jeddah. He came to see him in the hospital and when he saw how thin and pale he was, he grew concerned. The doctor also mentioned that Abdelkarim's immune system was low, which made him worry that his wife's brother might have a serious illness. But, as soon as the doctor informed him there was no need for him to stay at Salpêtrière Hospital any longer, Abdelkarim checked out and did his best to retrieve some bits and pieces of his life, though haunted by a dark feeling of emptiness and exile.

When he moved to Saudi Arabia, he took his anxiety with him. His brother-in-law seemed disappointed to see him and told him he should go back home. Abdelkarim's mother came up with a plan that involved getting him fired and cutting off his income. His sister would start the ball rolling by sending him a letter begging him to come home and when he asked her why, she would say that the family was going through a financial crisis. She would end her letter with some encouraging words that came verbatim from her mother: "*You are the only man left in the Azzam family. It is your duty to resurrect the family home!*"

Without much conviction, Abdelkarim tried at first to make a living on his own. But he soon learned he would never find a good job, and when the bank transfers stopped coming and he received a warning notice about not having paid his rent for three months, he realized it was over. After Valeria, his life just wasn't going to amount to much. It was like going down a tunnel of despair with no light at the end of it. Bertrand, who was planning to go to Somalia for several weeks to take photos of nothing but the beautiful dark-faced women there in their colorful clothes, carrying their babies as they walked, and who was the only person who knew the cause of Abdelkarim's decline, told him that some illnesses are best treated by a change in atmosphere. And so Abdelkarim organized a dinner party at his apartment. Everyone he invited—friends and pseudo-friends in Paris who helped take his mind off life without Valeria if only for a little while—all got drunk and sang the night away, sitting on the floor because Abdelkarim had sold his expensive black Chesterfield sofas through an ad he placed in a paper distributed at the metro station. It had taken him days to decide which of Valeria's belongings he wanted to keep and move to his apartment. At dawn the next day, he bid his final dinner guests goodbye with long embraces exaggerated by all the wine he'd drunk. They hugged him and warned him that if he didn't come back soon, they were going to get on a plane and surprise him right in his own "Mameluke city," as he always described it to anyone listening.

Abdelkarim took a flight the next day, lugging with him four large suitcases plus a carry-on for which he paid a huge fee for overages, even after a long dispute with the airport attendant. He made sure each bag was tagged properly, put on his sunglasses, and killed one last hour in the duty-free zone, in the opera and ballet movie section at the Virgin. On the plane, he decided to have some tranquilizers rather than Black Label. He declined the in-flight meal and slept the whole way to Beirut. After landing, he got in a taxi and finished his night's sleep during the ride north. He got to the house in the evening, with no need for anyone's help. His sister had mailed him a set of keys to the family house before he left Paris.

Spring had just begun. They arrived at ten o'clock, and the moment the taxi driver left, after helping him get his luggage into the house and setting it down in the middle of the salon, Abdelkarim went outside and stood in front of the house, inundated with nostalgia. He stood on the steps, leaned his head back, shut his eyes tight, and waited for the scent of the sea to reach him. With this exaggerated gesture of his, he relived a moment from his childhood, thirty years earlier, back when he was certain his father and mother would never die and thought that their house there in the gardens would be his first and last home. He recalled a scene that also took place at night, and in the month of April, too. But that night was a different kind of night. "Pitch black" as one might write on a school composition assignment. Darkness fraught with all sorts of danger, voices calling in the distance, snoring sounds, wailing sounds, intermittent whistling coming from the thick orchards that stretched as far as the eye could see. He and his sister were making noises and attributing them to wild animals. Then they would run to their father seated on the porch swing and jump into his lap in fright, competing for his affection. He put his finger to his lips, hushing them. All their talk was a distraction. "Smell the air," he says, and so they close their eyes and breathe in the scent of the orange blossoms that flooded the night air at the start of every spring. Many minutes go by while being cradled in their father's embrace, silent and sleepy in the warmth of his big body. They don't even notice their mother standing behind them, following the same daily ritual. She joins in with them before calling them inside because they had to get up early for school in the morning. They start moving, reluctantly, while he tells them how the old city souks get drenched in the fragrance of orange blossoms, how it reaches all that way, all the way to their old house. Abdelkarim told that whole story to Valeria and Bertrand and the others. He spiced it up for his listeners by adding that the fragrance reached all the way to the Mawlawi Whirling Dervish Monastery at the river's highest point, intoxicating the whirling dervishes whose supplications rose to the heavens, and everyone living in the area came out to their doorsteps to glorify God.

He tried to ascertain what he had left behind there, on a night marred only by the lanterns atop broken lampposts. It was a night filled with friendly and comforting voices, and so he lingered outside. He looked funny standing there, perfectly still, with his nose in the air. The only smell that reached him was the diesel exhaust coming from the passing taxis and busses, and the only sound was the rumble of the generator coming from the building next door. If he listened closely he could hear the chirps of some leftover crickets lost in the few scattered orange groves still remaining amid the jungle of buildings.

He spent the night sprawled out on his stomach on his bed, still wearing all his clothes and his shoes, with his feet hanging over the edge of the bed like when he went through bouts of anger in his adolescence. When he finally woke up very late the next morning, he turned onto his back, clasped his hands behind his head, and lay there in the dark not knowing where or why to begin. He didn't change his clothes or take a shower, to keep the smell of his previous life on his body as long as possible. He made do with the faint light creeping in from outside and two bars of dark chocolate he'd picked up at the airport in case of emergency. Then he spent the whole day keeping to himself, delaying getting up and trying to go back to sleep. He woke up in the morning to the sound of a door slamming and someone making noise in the kitchen. It was Intisar, Imm Mahmoud's daughter. He jumped out of bed and shook his head like a wet bird shaking water off its feathers.

"Open the windows!" he shouted into the distance in a frightening voice, as if he were suffocating. When he heard her opening one of the windows in the salon, he shouted again, "Open them all!"

Suddenly he remembered that the bonsai trees were still in his suitcase and would die there in the dark.

Intisar was a grown woman now. A beautiful woman. The same Intisar who as a young girl would sit in the kitchen all day long refusing to respond to anything anyone from the Azzam family said to her. It appeared her mother had warned her not to open her mouth for fear of what offensive things she might say. The same Intisar who had given him that shiny red candy apple, the one who used to go with her girlfriends and follow that old-timer who liked to decorate his clothes with wildflowers whenever he came back from the city. They would wait for him to go urinate in some corner where everyone could see him and then throw rocks at him and run away. The same Intisar whose poor mother threw up her hands in defeat after failing to stop her daughter from spewing swears and foul language. Now here she was, a grown woman, tending to the house as if she'd been born in it.

While helping him unpack the trees, her hand accidentally brushed against his. He looked deeply into her eyes, inspired by the hope she might be there with him every day. He unpacked the shears and the plant food from the suitcase. He inspected a broken branch and some wilting leaves and then placed the trees in a sunny spot. He lined them up very carefully, the same way Valeria had placed them in her apartment. The Indian lilac first, then the tea tree, followed by the Japanese maple, and on the far left the wild azarole. He unpacked his clothes, his books, and all his Parisian spoils. Intisar went home to the American Quarter, leaving Abdelkarim alone with his thoughts. He imagined Valeria pregnant with his child and dreamt up new ways to contact her. Then he unpacked her skirts —pink ones, blue ones, white ones; and her corsets and her cosmetics—all sorts of tubes and little brushes; and her wigs and eyelash curlers, all her shoes, her hair ribbons, her tights, her tiny underpants, her bras, her headbands, her gold tiaras, the black raincoat she was wearing the first time he saw her, the photo Bertrand took of her, her bottles of perfume she used after practice and before performances and on the lovers' bed. He placed them all in the closet in the bedroom next-door to his and locked the door.

Two days later, he went out into the city. He took the route the school busses follow on rainy mornings, avoiding the speeding cars while walking his usual delicate way in his slippery shoes. He explored the narrow streets. He was struck by the wrinkled faces of passersby on the sidewalk and an unending cacophony of sounds coming from some unknown source. Some little bare feet came up from behind—a tribe of Bedouins with their women who swarmed the pedestrians passing by the Ottoman clock tower. They approached him. Little brown hands tugged at his sleeves, begging for alms.

"For the love of God…"

A skinny young man carrying a sack and wearing a bright green nose and plastic green glasses came along making bird-chirping sounds with something in his hands. He was selling the noses and glasses and bird-chirping gadgets. He had sad eyes behind his funny mask as he quickly moved straight ahead. He chirped haphazardly with his plastic green nose up in the air, hoping the rest would happen by chance. Maybe a little boy would whine for his mother to buy him a set so he could imitate him. But he was running farther and farther into the distance, with no children in the streets to slow him down. The streets were desolate, as if grey dust had rained down all over them, all over everything, except for a few scattered spots of blue or dark red on the storefronts and the dismantled wooden window frames.

He stopped before the labyrinth of shops that had sprung up where the Frères' school had stood and where he'd spent half his life. He spied out the spot where the library had been, whose entire collection he might have actually read, up above an Islamic apparel shop where an unveiled salesgirl was standing in the doorway. The hunting gear shop was gone, along with its new rifle display case. The barber they called "Rico" was still there, next door to where the school was. Abdelkarim makes a point to walk by and catches a glimpse of him sitting in his rotating chair—the same red leather one—with his head rolled back, taking a nap before noon while there weren't many customers. His mouth was wide open, showing where half his front teeth were missing. A fat man on a small motor scooter heaving under his weight brushes up against Abdelkarim from behind as he tries to wheedle his way through traffic. He has an open crate attached to the back of the bike with something heaped in it resembling a dead cat. The trash bins are overflowing with garbage, and the odor mingles with the smell of the river and the smell of flavored tobacco coming from the hookah pipes two muscular young men sitting on the edge of the sidewalk are puffing on. One of them, the one with a tattoo on his shoulder, wears a shirt that says, "I love the Los Angeles Lakers." They're eyeing Abdelkarim and making gestures about his slender physique. A woman carrying a sick, scrawny baby with his eyes closed—like a piece of cloth to wave at passersby—waves him in Abdelkarim's face. A vendor who calls himself "Abu Fu'ara," Poor Man's Friend, spreads out a forest of used goods. He stands on his wooden trunk, holds up a pair of shoes and a shirt that he fishes out from the pile of clothes and flings into the air. In a scratchy voice, he advertises his low prices through a megaphone he's holding in his other hand.

Abdelkarim goes back home, shoulders drooping like a wounded bird. The next day he has to face his cousin Riyad, the family's heir politician, who shows up unannounced. He gives his cousin a long embrace and gets a bit dizzy from the strong and sticky cologne he's wearing.

"I don't know your phone number," he says.

"I don't have a cell phone," Abdelkarim answers, at which his cousin curls his lips in astonishment. He came in an escort car with tinted windows, accompanied by two armed bodyguards carrying revolvers in plain sight. They look all around in an exaggerated manner, and his cousin keeps giving them trivial tasks to do. Riyad offers his condolences for his uncle Abdallah and plops down in his armchair without asking permission.

"This is where he used to sit," he says as he sits down.

He asks Abdelkarim about his time away, which Abdelkarim doesn't know how to respond to except to mumble a few phrases. His cousin tries to revive some sort of conspiratorial kinship between them by telling little anecdotes from their past. He reminds him of his infatuation with the blonde French sisters and how he used to send them poems written on scraps of paper.

But Abdelkarim appears to have forgotten all that and just smiles nervously, as though he's become a new man his cousin lacks the curiosity to figure out. And so, for the remainder of the visit, he changes his line of attack, limiting the conversation to things that don't require a response from Abdelkarim. He sits with one leg crossed over the other, swinging his foot in the air, staring at his shiny shoes and black silk socks. Abdelkarim, sitting across from him, shows clear signs of nervousness. He blinks uncontrollably and his neck muscles are tight. He holds his face in his hands, listening to his cousin's diatribe of complaints. The city's dead. It wakes up late and by eight turns into a ghost town. At one time, this same city had fought off the French Mandate, and it stood in solidarity with every Arab cause: for the Algerian revolution, against the Baghdad Pact. Everyone, without exception, went out into the streets the day Nasser resigned, and in 1948 it was one of this city's men who led the Arab Salvation Army for the liberation of Palestine. But nowadays, the city couldn't be bothered. During elections, the rich went around buying votes—rich people with fortunes amassed by questionable means.

Abdelkarim calls to Intisar and asks her to bring some coffee, hoping to put a damper on his cousin's rant. Intisar's attractive figure doesn't go unnoticed by Riyad, who gives her a long stare before suddenly changing the topic from politics to mourning the death of all the local cinemas who'd closed their doors one after the other. "Cinema Metropole, the Colorado, the Romance, the Roxy," he lists them off, striving to remember as far back as possible. Abdelkarim holds his tongue, trying to avoid saying something he might regret. He moves from one sofa to another as a way of relieving his anxiety. Meanwhile, his cousin goes on about how impossible it was to go out and do anything remotely entertaining at night, and how even if you wanted to invite some friends out to dinner you had to go to one of the Christian towns. And if you wanted a nice suit, you had to go to Beirut. The Evangelical schools had deserted the city and the Christian population had dwindled. In the past, they used to carry their icons and do their processions out in the streets while the shopkeepers stood in their doorways, respectfully watching them go by. But then the fundamentalists took control of the mosques and found a way to kick out any preacher who abstained from calling for jihad. They draped their women in black *niqab*, called people infidels, and forbade them from anything unsacred. They made threats against women's hairstylists and prohibited male doctors from treating female patients. They publicly berated anyone who broke the fast and cracked down on alcohol consumption by stopping people at checkpoints at the city limits and forcing anyone with suspicious-smelling breath out of the car. They accumulated huge amounts of cash in their personal bank accounts, hired a gang of armed bodyguards, and sent young men to fight at fronts they never returned from.

Abdelkarim stood up, hoping his cousin might decide it was time to leave, but unfortunately he remained seated and went on eulogizing his city at length, as if to trivialize its value as a way to compensate Abdelkarim for the prestige he had missed out on. He didn't stop until his phone alarm went off, reminding him of an important appointment, and so he made his apologies and went on his way, reassured that his cousin was in no way planning to compete with him politically. Immediately after his clamorous exit with his entourage of overexcited bodyguards, Abdelkarim cleared the air with the sound of Montserrat Caballé, a despairing lover from *La Traviata*, whose voice reverberated into the evening. The blaring music made Intisar tremble in fear. She soon learned to recognize that whenever that sound filled every corner of the house it meant Abdelkarim Bey al-Azzam had plunged once again into one of his dark moods.

Listening to the voices of female singers filling the house while he pruned his bonsai trees became an addiction, one of the side effects of his return flight from Paris. It was a kind of therapy. A way to reconnect with years of lost happiness, happiness that might suddenly resurface. There remained a tiny thread of a chance that the phone would ring one day and he would hear Valeria's voice with its deep timbre. She would call him from wherever she was, and let him hear the cooing sounds of their newborn child. He would sell the old family house and run to her. After all, hadn't he given her the phone number to the house when he came for his father's funeral? She had insisted on writing it down so she could check on him and make sure he was okay during his short absence. She never did call, though, proving to him once again that he had good reason to think that the moment he was out of sight she slipped into another world, the same world he found himself in every time she got on the phone with a family member and started frowning and speaking nervously in her native language. That was the world that swallowed her up in the end. A place Abdelkarim had been banished from, just as he had always been banished from the places where the people he loved lived.

He took down the expensive wine-colored Bokhara tapestry that was hanging on the wall in the salon and hung her picture in its place. It was the enlarged photograph Bertrand had taken of her, in black and white, in which she is standing on tiptoes, with her head—decorated with a bow—leaning against her raised arm. Her slender, inclined body, in its pure whiteness, is wrapped in a tight shirt with black dots tied at the chest and a transparent tutu. It was as though in the empty space Bertrand had drawn a letter from the alphabet or a giant musical note. A flash of light against the jet-black background made it possible, if one looked carefully, to make out a row of tiny ballerinas undulating in a veiled fog in the distance. He hung the photograph in front of the chair he sat in every day, from where her sad eyes could look back at him whenever he raised his head in her direction. Having her in his line of vision helped allay his feelings of longing for her and the wild imaginings that danced through his mind.

Intisar didn't ask him about the woman in the picture, and not without a certain level of concealed jealousy she thought that despite the enchanting eyes, she was too skinny, "scrawny," and thought Abdelkarim deserved better. She chalked it up to a growing list of Abdelkarim's peculiarities and tried her best to help him manage the burden of visitors who kept unexpectedly showing up at the house. It seemed that the news of Abdelkarim al-Azzam's return had secretly found its way into circles of the needy, people who were not discouraged from seeking out his charity despite having been told that the man of the house did not engage in public affairs. The whole city came to see him. One time an extremely garrulous old woman came to visit who told him she had to take four different taxis to get to his house from her distant village, just as she had so often done in the past to visit his father—who never refused a request. She asked for a glass of water, which Intisar brought to her with indifference. Then the old woman pulled out a prescription; it had passed through so many hands she'd had it plastic-coated. In a nutshell, she was suffering from an acute illness and couldn't afford the necessary treatment. Abdelkarim gave her some money, and later that afternoon, along came a man wearing an old striped suit and a necktie. Without introducing himself, he congratulated Abdelkarim for his safe return. Then he sat silently for a long time before grabbing a tissue and bursting into tears. He went on to tell an unending story, with plenty of sobs in between, that appeared to have no beginning, middle, or end. He started out complaining about a sheikh from a Sufi brotherhood, who had money coming out of his ears and knew the Sultan of Brunei and how he had predicted that one day the sea would flow onto the dry land, which was exactly what happened. So, the Sultan rewarded him handsomely.

"But we are poor people," said the man all of a sudden. Abdelkarim supposed he must not be right in the head, and was very strange, indeed, because he immediately switched to talking about some man he called "Yunis the German." He was a tall, blond man with blue eyes who knew Arabic well and embraced Islam. He roamed the mountains carrying a long walking stick and no one knew where he came from.

"What do we have to do with those people?"

The man was scattering words all over the place. Meanwhile, Intisar looked on from the kitchen, where only Abdelkarim could see her from where he was sitting in his father's armchair. She gestured to him with raised eyebrows, to tell him the man was a liar; she knew who he was and Abdelkarim should not be fooled by him. He enjoyed this complicity with Intisar. The man continued his story, saying that the German and the Sufi sheikh convinced some young men to escape up into the mountains because the sea was going to rise and cover the city. Cyprus was going to disappear under water. They left their work and their families and carried tents and food with them and set up camp in the bitter cold of the mountains. They did physical training exercises, prayed, and followed an 'orientation' regiment until one day some weaponry arrived. They had been preparing for the flood that was going to drown the mountain and ended up going to battle instead. Then a messenger came to them who ordered them to prepare an attack on New Year's Eve, the last night of the year 2000.

"The world will live one thousand years, but not two!" the messenger told them, while Yunis the German nodded his head in agreement. They wrapped their heads and faces in kufiyahs, dangled Qurans around their necks, and set out down the mountain. They clashed with the army and were chased down by patrol cars and police dogs. They split up and those who died, died, and those who were arrested were arrested. The man started bawling again, swearing that his second son was innocent but got sentenced to two years in prison.

"It's true, my eldest son was with them, I don't deny it. Here's his picture," he said as he opened his worn-out leather wallet and pulled out the papers and cards that were in it until he found the picture of a teenager looking into the camera lens with puffy eyes.

"This one died. He was shot in the heart. After he died, his mother got cancer. The sheikh left the country, and the German disappeared just as he had appeared in the first place—out of nowhere. My other son has finished serving his sentence and needs only to pay his fine." He blew his nose loudly and swore he didn't have a single lira to his name to pay for his son's release, and that apart from God, he had no one to turn to other than this fine household.

That story was well worth the small price Abdelkarim paid, but the visits that ensued were even more comical or difficult to manage, like the Bedouin family from the Akkar plain who wanted to obtain citizenship, but because their parents and grandparents hadn't applied for it, they got placed into the category known as "Undisclosed Status." They didn't know who to turn to for help with their case, which started all the way back in 1932. Or like the man wishing to have his brother transferred to a barracks closer to his birthplace after having served in the army two years in the South, at the Israeli border.

Abdelkarim felt cooped up in the house during the day, and so he went to visit his maternal aunt. She had always been his oasis, since he was a little boy. All the doting and gifts came from his mother's side of the family. She gave him a warm embrace and made him stay for dinner. Afterward, she made coffee and invited him out onto the porch. They sat together on the swing, drinking coffee and taking in the view. From where they were on the tenth floor they could see the barren land that stretched all the way to the sea.

"There's not a single tree left!" Abdelkarim exclaimed, scanning the landscape in a semi-circle from north to south in search of the dark green belt that used to gird the city like a mother's embrace, around all three sides.

They uprooted everything in less than a week. They brought in bulldozers and then sold the tree limbs as firewood. All those groves, the level and winding ones, that narrowed or widened, whose areas overlapped, and were bordered by streams and demarcated by fences...The civil engineers divided them up into perfectly square or rectangular lots. They mapped out where roads would be and common spaces and argued over the percentage of built-up land. No one cared about the orange groves, because the price of the land had skyrocketed. Each grove had had a name, and before Friday prayers, assessors would come to Al-Awayni Café and call out the names of the various orange groves to *dammanehs*, the crop guarantors sitting at the café puffing on hookahs. This would set the orange grove auction into motion. Keys to the groves would be distributed to participants so they could go and evaluate the potential harvest. Then they would come back the following Friday and with a simple nod of the head would win the auction and their names would be recorded in the ledger. But there was always a chance of stormy weather, or an early frost, that could ruin the crop, the traders, and the *dammanehs* in one fell swoop. One unexpected blow could wipe out a hundred harvests. And harvesting was women's work. They'd sit on the ground, wipe the brown specks from the fruit, and sort them into quality grades. Then came wrapping them in paper and packing them in crates, and finally they were carried off on wooden donkey carts to market or onto freight trains, or to cargo ships moored at the port; those oranges that went out to sea were called *marakbi*, or boater oranges.

His aunt puts him in a state of bliss. She knows everything about oranges, lists the varieties one by one, lauds their qualities, knows their seasons. The *sukkari* is sweet and is the first to come into season the first of November, before the winter rains begin. It's followed by the smaller *afandi* and its newcomer competitor, the clementine. It can easily be peeled by hand and leaves a fragrance on your fingers that you don't want to wipe off. The navel orange is the star of midwinter, coming into season around the first of the new year. It's a newly grafted variety, but has surpassed all the older varieties. Then there's the *baladi* followed by the Jaffa orange that comes in early March, along with the blood red *mawardi*. The Valencia is a straggler, and last but not least is the *khitmali*, the end of season variety. Lemons, on the other hand, are available all year round.

She talks about orange blossom jam, made from the little white flower petals that are plucked one by one and removed one hour after distillation. And that over there is bitter orange marmalade, and when it comes to orange blossom water, the best kind comes from the unirrigated orange groves. His aunt describes these and points toward the south, where the rivulets from the river didn't reach, as if the trees were still standing there in front of her. And her reverie doesn't stop there. She switches from the oranges to the local "families" and how anyone who didn't own an orange grove in the grove region—the western part or the southern part—was not one of the city's native sons. He'd have been a newcomer, going only one or two generations back. She tells the story, making sure not to leave out the names of the families, listing them one by one, while Abdelkarim surrenders to the sweet sound of her voice. There are only two or three families who were known for owning olive groves, which had been handed down over the generations from father to son. She speaks as if the world was still as it was, and then she realizes that things have changed. Abdelkarim takes this as his cue to get up to leave before she can start the diatribe of complaints he guesses would include a painful nostalgia for the school she went to and a listing one by one of all the nuns who taught her, with their Italian names, which she still remembered after all these years.

He came home to find a young man at his house. He could not have been more than twenty years old, tall, with disheveled hair. He was glued to Valeria's photograph, running his fingers over her face as if to feel the softness of her cheek. As soon as he heard Abdelkarim come in, he quickly pulled his hand back, like someone getting caught hitting on someone else's girl. After managing to regain his composure, he looked Abdelkarim in the eye without lowering his sharp, black, inquisitive stare until Intisar stepped in to defuse the tension.

"This is my son, Ismail," she broke in. "His grandfather served at your grandfather's side, and now he will serve at yours."

She had whisked him away from the American Quarter hoping the police would forget about him after the election poster incident.

Ismail brought a chair outside and sat at the front door watching the cars and people pass by on the street. He chased off a young man carrying a leather briefcase who, after walking along the fence, had found an opening in the row of trees and was peering inside at the house. He claimed to be a lawyer representing some people interested in buying the house. Being a single-story house with ground-level parking in an area surrounded by ten-story apartment buildings, it was a last bastion of sorts, something building contractors would pay a lot of money for.

At dusk, Intisar returned to the American Quarter, leaving Ismail alone with Abdelkarim.

"Behave yourself," she advised him. "You sleep here," she added, pointing to the sofa she'd made up for him in the kitchen. That first night he kept himself quiet, though Abdelkarim could sense his presence despite his being out of sight.

Intisar's mother had been a part of the family—she and Hasan al-Owayk. The family had quarreled in front of Imm Mahmoud, said things about their relatives they wouldn't normally say in front of people. They'd all conspired with her, Abdelkarim included, in his case against his sour-tempered wife. Then Intisar inherited her mother's place in the household. She was thirty-seven, with four children, a husband who never showed his face, and a figure that was still a very inviting sight. She resembled her mother in many ways— same voice, same posture, same way of bending down to mop the floor, and even the way she would surrender to her fatigue and sit to rest for a few minutes before packing up her things and heading back home. He often gazed at her face whenever she slipped unawares into a silent, serious mood. She had black eyes, full lips, a long slender nose. Abdelkarim imagined that if his photographer friend Bertrand were to catch sight of Intisar, if he were to tell him about her childhood and her marriage and her living conditions, Bertrand would go to her neighborhood to find her with his camera. He would capture her and her natural grace in some chance moment, sitting all alone on one of those high stairways momentarily empty of pedestrians, or leaning against some stained and faded wall temporarily lit up by her expressive form. Abdelkarim was always conscious of her presence in the house, whether she was working in front of him in the salon or even in the kitchen, from where the familiar and comforting sounds still reached him.

Her son Ismail, on the other hand, always made his presence known loudly and clearly. He explored the house as if touring a museum. He followed Abdelkarim's every move with utmost curiosity, made sudden noises, as if he were forcing himself to keep quiet, merely to do as his mother told him. But he couldn't control himself forever. After a few days, a question finally leaked out of him just out of the blue.

"Why do you keep cutting these trees' roots?" He had been eyeing Abdelkarim ever since he got his gardening tools out and started attending to one of the bonsai trees.

"To stunt their growth!" Abdelkarim answered, smiling.

"And why do you bend the branches back?"

"So they don't get too thick!"

"What's the point of these trees?" he asked, broadening his line of questioning.

"They teach me patience."

"Is that all?"

"And wisdom."

Two words that didn't exactly strike a chord of understanding with his young friend, who kept pushing the issue. "But why don't you want them to grow?"

"Why do you *want* them to grow?"

"That's how God created them."

"If they grow, they'll escape to the outdoors. They won't fit inside the house anymore."

"That's against nature!"

"I don't like nature!"

"If you had a child, would you stop him from growing, too?"

"That's why I don't have children…" Abdelkarim said remembering pregnant Valeria.

It had gotten very late and Abdelkarim had drunk too many glasses of whiskey. "I've got it," he kept repeating to himself. "Yes, I've got it now. I don't like nature!"

The fencing match ended quickly that night after Abdelkarim offered to give Ismail one of the bonsai trees. He told him to choose one, and without consideration, his young friend pointed to the wild azarole with all its little fruits, perhaps because it was the only one that had any fruit on it.

After that the floodgates were open on the conversation between them. Abdelkarim initiated it the next day and in the days that followed. He bombarded Ismail with prying questions: Where did he sleep? Where did he eat? What books did he read? Did he go regularly to the mosque to pray? Did he have friends? Was he interested in travel? Did he listen to music? Ismail told him about his uncle and how there wasn't a place in the world he hadn't visited. He told him about the postcards he received from his uncle's summer vacations—the Leaning Tower of Pisa, the bronze naked mermaid statue. They talked late into the night, delving into every topic under the sun. Ismail wanted to know how Abdelkarim acquired the dwarfed trees, so he told him about Valeria. That was the first time he ever spoke to another human being about her.

"I loved her. I gave her an orange tree and she wrote my name on it. She took it with her wherever it is that she went."

"Did she love you?"

"I don't know, but I do know that I will never love anyone else my whole life…"

Ismail sat quietly, out of respect for this soul baring he never expected from the master of the house. Then he released his own tongue from its chains, and without any reason or any prompting, revealed to Abdelkarim that he and his buddies in the American Quarter had shot off fireworks on September 11, the day of the attacks on New York and Washington, D.C., and wrote graffiti praising the heroes who flew the airplanes. And Abdelkarim, for his part, described to his young companion, in great detail, the place he believed his ballerina girlfriend was now living—somewhere in the suburbs of Belgrade with its tidy old houses with blue windows and camellia flowers. From there Abdelkarim turned to talking about Valeria's mother who fell head over heels in love with a circus performer and prayed he wouldn't fall from his tightrope, and then about the Serbs and their obsession with family honor and having a balcony overlooking where the Danube and the Sava rivers meet.

By midnight, all their inhibitions were set free. Abdelkarim took a break from fantasizing about Bucharest, a city he'd never seen in his life, and invited Ismail to join him in a drink. After some initial hesitation, Ismail accepted and brought the whiskey glasses and chopped the ice himself. He started off with a big swig of the strong whiskey, squeezing his eyes shut as he swallowed. Then he proceeded to tell Abdelkarim how he had torn down the election posters, some of which belonged to Abdelkarim's cousin, and how he was the one who splattered paint on them, and how the caption said, "Riyad al-Azzam, Epitome of Nobility." Abdelkarim exploded in laughter, overjoyed by what Ismail had done and wished he could tell the story to his sister. Then Intisar's son told him how he and his buddies extended their mischief out into the city streets at night. They took amphetamines before going after billboards of women in skimpy lingerie. Meanwhile, Abdelkarim reminisced about the orange groves. With some difficulty, he stood up and started reciting poetry, or something he seemed to think was poetry. Ismail couldn't make heads or tails of it except a few words here and there having to do with "salt" and "Andalus" and "blood." With arms flailing in a theatrical gesture, he finished off his poem with a final line from Mahmoud Darwish:

And here at this spot a wind skidded off the horse's back

The whiskey having gotten to his head, too, Ismail takes his turn raving in a loud voice, threatening those who would persecute the poor native sons of this town. Their voices rise up and their delirious ravings intermingle, while neither one hears what the other is saying. Abdelkarim teeters and finally stumbles to the ground, bursting into tears. Ismail helps him back onto his feet and gets him to his bedroom. He helps him into bed and puts a pillow under his head. Thinking Abdelkarim has fallen asleep, Ismail tries to get up to go to the kitchen, but Abdelkarim grabs him by the arm, begging him to stay. The drunk and dizzy Ismail props himself up with his back against the headboard and Abdelkarim lays his head on Ismail's chest. They stop talking and all that can be heard is the sound of their labored breathing. During the night, Abdelkarim wraps his arms around Ismail in his sleep and they stay that way, in a sort of embrace, until morning. When Ismail wakes up, he untangles himself from Abdelkarim's embrace and goes to the bathroom. He splashes his face with water, twice, and stares at himself for a long time in the mirror. Not wanting to face Abdelkarim when he wakes up in a little while, Ismail packs up his few belongings and flees the Azzam house, without looking back.

5

Early one Sunday morning, Sitara arrived at the Hindu Temple located on the ground floor of a building on the main highway a few kilometers outside the capital. She reached the Temple before the expected arrival of the maids and gas station and shopping center attendants who would be streaming in, in groups, to attend the weekly prayer service. She'd gotten there bright and early to tidy up the place and prepare the weekly advisory talk she gave to the young women about their financial rights and the proper procedures to follow in case of mistreatment.

Just as she was trying to choose the best words to summarize for her audience the interview she'd conducted with the Sri Lankan Ambassador two days earlier, she lifted her eyes from the page and noticed a young man outside the window wearing a grease-stained blue uniform who was in quite a hurry to get out of a small delivery vehicle with the name of the German newspaper *Die Welt* written on it. He looked right and left several times before dropping a bag into the metal trash bin in front of the temple. Then he turned around and just as quickly got back behind the steering wheel and took off north.

Her suspicions raised, Sitara rushed out to the street, waving her hands in the air. A traffic officer on motorcycle traveling in the opposite direction on his way home at the end of a long Saturday night shift that he'd spent pulling over party-goers and drunk drivers, saw her. She shouted to him, pointing fearfully at the area in front of the temple, and so the officer took the first exit and headed back in her direction. In the few minutes it took him to arrive, he'd contacted the closest police station. Internal security officers arrived minutes later. They blocked the Sri Lankan and Indian maids and laborers from reaching the temple, and immediately evacuated apartment residents from the upper stories of the building. They also stopped all traffic on both sides of the highway in anticipation of the military expert's arrival. When he got there, he approached the trash bin, opened the bag, and suddenly backed away. He started running and waving his arms for everyone to get as far back as possible because the bomb had a timer attached to it, couldn't be defused, and might go off any second. And that is precisely what happened. Suddenly there was a loud boom; dust and red flames flew up in the air, windows shattered, bits of metal went flying everywhere, landing on cars parked nearby on both sides of the highway. Some soldiers and curious bystanders were wounded by the debris. Sitara didn't know much Arabic, but she succeeded in identifying the type of vehicle she had seen by pointing out a similar model parked in the area. She also identified the color of the car and described the driver's clothing. Thanks to her description, the officer was able to call into headquarters asking for the arrest of a man fitting the description, "The driver of a white Rapid model vehicle with foreign inscription on it…"

The culprit was easily apprehended at a checkpoint set up along the northern route and was taken in for questioning at the Internal Security headquarters, where the inspector reassured him there had been no casualties as a result of his crime, as if his mother had prayed for him. He might get away with three years in prison if he confessed. The suspect admitted to the crime, which he claimed was carried out "in retaliation for the persecution that Muslims in India were being subjected to at the hands of the 'Buddhists.'" Not realizing that the intended target had been a Hindu temple, the investigator asked the perpetrator what his motives were, prompting him to speak at great length about the necessity to stand in solidarity with Muslims around the world. He concluded his speech, after feeling with some certainty that the investigator was a Muslim, by quoting a verse from Surat al-Baqara:

> *"Prescribed for you is fighting, though it be hateful to you. Yet it may happen that you will hate a thing which is better for you…"*

The investigator cut him short with a sharp slap in the face and pressed him for the names of all his accomplices.

His accomplices in the American Quarter operated under the guise of the "Islamic Guidance Association." It was an organization that started out by opening a school and a small religious bookstore. Then they inaugurated a clinic and gave out wheelchairs to the crippled. They all wore identical short *jalabiyas*, in accordance with a *hadith* that encouraged pious believers to wear clothing "that reached the calf." Eventually they were able to get their hands on the Attar Mosque, which Sheikh Abdellatif had barred them from for years. Their first step was to boycott the sheikh's Friday sermon and instead cross to the other side of the river to attend Friday prayers at the Tawheed

Mosque near the Gold Souks. Their war on the sheikh was not easy. People loved him and the way his boisterous laughter at some witty joke he'd just told preceded him. Many would bend to kiss his hand, although he would pull it away and pat them on the head or shoulder instead. He'd retired from school teaching and spent his day popping in and out of one shop after another, never sitting down anywhere despite all the invitations. He grieved for the Arabs and Arabism, reciting by heart long excerpts of poems by Ahmad Shawqi and Muhammad Mahdi al-Jawahiri. And he'd mock "this era of 'midgets' we're living in," and whisper in the ears of those he trusted that these men with the long beards were the epitome of lowliness. He would ask young men who came to meet him about their family names and was always saying that the newcomers who'd come to the city from the villages and countryside outnumbered the original inhabitants. He harbored no feelings of ill will toward them, but rather sympathized with their poverty. He'd whisper in this one's ear and chuckle with another. People in need sought him out for help, because they knew he had clout with government deputies and important city officials. He had access to them whenever he wanted; they never refused a request from him and he never asked for anything for himself.

He remained there at the neighborhood mosque, and every Friday people from all over sought him out and never missed a service or one of his sermons. The Attar Mosque filled up with men not typical of the American Quarter of old: doctors, engineers, and judges dressed in neckties and fancy suits; and even some high-ranking officers came wearing their official uniforms if their leave time allowed them the chance. Some were his former pupils and others had bonded in friendship while marching arm-in-arm at the forefront of national demonstrations. He spoke out against celebrating the

September 11 attacks on the Twin Towers in New York, and likewise criticized in the harshest terms the American invasion of Iraq. But the calls for young men to go and fight did not please him. One day he stood up in his pulpit, clasped his hands together, and exclaimed point-blank, that "the most important jihad is man's struggle against himself, the jihad of the soul and its reform." Some mumblings rose up from among the "Islamic Guidance" contingency, and one of them—maybe even Yasin al-Shami himself—shouted loudly and rudely, "And what about the enemies of God and Islam?"

To this, Sheikh Abellatif sharply responded that Islam's most destructive enemies were "certain Muslims," clearly referring to them. At that they stormed out of the mosque and didn't return, until Sheikh Abdellatif broke his hip. As he was descending the quarter's steps one rainy morning on his way back from the butcher shop carrying the filet his wife sent him to pick up, his foot slipped and he fell hard to the ground. The doctors all concurred that surgery at his age was ill-advised and that the only treatment for him was bed rest. The moment news of his fall spread around the area, his devotees stopped coming to pray at the Attar Mosque and went instead to various new neighborhood mosques that had been built with donations from rich men who'd been among the first to go abroad and make money from oil in the Emirates. Nevertheless, they were often exasperated by some of the sermons of this or that sheikh who'd appeared out of nowhere.

And that was how the Islamic Guidance Association took over the Attar Mosque. The sheikhs put up a banner at the entrance, with "Guidance Mosque" written in bright red letters. Just like that, the Mameluke mosque that Emir Sayf el-Din had erected in the fourteenth century got transformed into a recruiting station for young soldiers they sent out for jihad. It was during that time when Ismail started working at the kohl-eyed Yasin al-Shami's bakery. Yasin was the first man Ismail had ever seen who put kohl around his eyes like a woman, and in fact no one in the quarter remembered any other man before him who'd used kohl like that except for a Sufi sheikh who'd rented an apartment in the area and tried to establish a group of mystic chant singers but died before getting it off the ground.

At first Yasin didn't try to guide him on the right path. He'd just leave a copy out on the counter of an Islamic magazine that was hand-delivered to him from a group he'd met during his years in exile. Ismail wouldn't do much more than flip through the pages without giving it much thought. Al-Shami was unsure where to begin with him. He asked Ismail whether he was practicing his religion and found him to be quite lackadaisical about it. He'd leave the bakery at the end of his shift and go out recklessly into the streets. Yasin started to doubt his original intuition toward Ismail and regretted hiring him, until one time when Ismail asked him about the Bab al-Hadid massacre.

"Your father knows," he answered. "He was at the Center that night. Maybe he doesn't want to tell you about it."

"No, he told me and showed me where."

It was there that Yasin al-Shami's life had begun, too. Before that, nothing worth mentioning ever happened to him. His brother was killed in it. They summoned him at dawn, the morning after the Bab al-Hadid massacre, to come down from his third floor apartment and present himself. His wife held him back and his children blocked the doorway trying to stop him from going out, but he thought he was safe since he hadn't been involved in the fighting. He'd lived in the quarter his whole life, and even though he loved Sheikh Imad, he never took up arms or joined him in his battle. He never even stepped foot in his office. And so his brother went downstairs, while his wife and children went out on the balcony, only to watch from above with their own eyes as the Mukhabarat officer shot him the moment he stepped outside the building to surrender.

"And what about you?"

"They only arrested me, since they'd killed my brother."

He quiets down when a late customer enters the bakery, rousing Ismail's curiosity even more. The next day, just before closing time, Yasin takes advantage of the lull in customers in the bakery at that time in the afternoon, to count the cash drawer and organize it. Then he sits down, pressing his hands on his hips, and asks Ismail to remind him where he'd left off in his story.

"First they blindfolded me and didn't ask me anything. They made me lay flat on my belly on a wooden plank that had a hinge in the middle and then they raised me up with chains, locking me inside the folded plank. Before they started to question me, they snapped two vertebrae in my back, sending me screaming in pain so bad I wanted to die."

He told all the details of his ordeal, how they put him in solitary confinement for six months, completely forgetting him for weeks. Then they'd go back to him and sit him in the "German chair," a metal seat causing severe stress to the spine, neck, and other limbs, to be interrogated. They wanted him to spill the names of everyone he knew in Bab al-Hadid. At first, he gave them the names of people he knew were dead, and if they checked and found out a certain person was dead, then al-Shami would act like it was a big surprise to him. In the end, they tried to get the names by torturing him with electric shocks.

"And did you give them names?"

"I knew that any name I gave them would mean that man would be brought there to face the same fate as me. I started praying, praying I'd stay alive, praying for God to grant me patience."

He never prayed before ending up in prison. In his youth, he joined a socialist organization that didn't put much stock in religion. In prison he tried to get a copy of the Quran, but they wouldn't give him one. They slapped him for asking. Then one day, God sent him an angel from heaven, a prisoner in the adjacent cell who knew the Quran by heart. He chanted the verses from behind the wall while al-Shami repeated after him. For months, perhaps, he instructed him, though al-Shami never saw the other prisoner's face.

"You never saw his face?" Ismail asked, his eyes suddenly black with disbelief.

"I never saw him at all. But his voice was pure and sweet. And I knew that whenever his voice grew faint or quavered that he'd been beaten and tortured. But he always completed his recitation, and repeated. Both our lives became entirely dependent on God's holy verses. But then suddenly he went silent, disappeared. In vain I called to him and recited the verses he'd taught me, hoping he would repeat after me, but I got no response. They'd taken him and I think they sentenced him to death."

After that, Yasin continued to pray on his own, repeating what parts he had memorized, and whenever they heard him chanting they would curse him and take him out for punishment. They pulled out all the fingernails of his right hand, and then when they were finally convinced they couldn't get any more out of him, they dumped him into a communal cell that had only one toilet. The ordeal of waiting his turn in the morning was like going from one kind of torture to a new one. Quite often one of the prisoners would not be able to hold himself and would soil his clothes.

"They transferred me from one prison to another. I saw women and children. I heard countless voices screaming in pain and degradation."

The following Friday they closed the bakery, and for the first time Ismail felt a sense of pride as he walked to the Attar Mosque beside Yasin al-Shami whose body heaved with each step because of his broken back. After prayers, he accompanied him for the first time to the Islamic Guidance Center. And that is how, on that afternoon, tracing a path of just a few hundreds meters between Sufi Hill and the Carpentry Souks, they delineated the triangle within which Ismail Muhsin would spend the next months of his new life: turning off the oven and cleaning it out once there were no more loaves to be baked, kneeling to perform "compensatory" prostrations, praying at the mosque and staying there in solitude between noon and Maghreb prayers, then finishing the day volunteering in the various charitable activities provided by the Center.

They gave him a tape recording of the Quran being chanted and a small cassette player with headphones to go with it so he could get his fill of the Quran without interruption, on condition he never used it to play any other cassette of any kind. They permitted him to access the internet on the center's computer and gave him a list of all the Islamic sites he could visit. He met a sheikh visiting from the Comoros Islands who was always smiling and spoke Arabic with an accent that was unfamiliar to Ismail. And whenever that sheikh received emergency phone calls from "abroad," as he said, he would speak French fluently like a native. He had come to tell them that jihad was no longer a collective duty, but an individual duty, considering the level of aggression the nation of Islam was being subjected to in Iraq, which could not be repelled without the help of all Muslims, no matter how close or far away they were. And he would always return to the same verse: *"Prescribed for you is fighting, though it be hateful to you."*

And then follow it with another: *"Go forth, light and heavy! Struggle in God's way with your possessions and your selves."*

Then, to conclude, anyone voicing a desire to assist in the cause was referred to "Brother" Abu Musab, who didn't attend such orientation meetings.

The Islamic Guidance Association soon grew very popular. It was heavily funded, people said, and its offices expanded so much they occupied an entire three-story building. People came to it from villages near and far. They gave Ismail the job of receiving visitors on the ground floor and directing them to the appropriate office. In that capacity, he saw the people as they arrived and heard their requests. One was a man who lifted his clothing to reveal a festering wound on his waist; he was asking for medicine after being refused emergency treatment at all the hospitals. And there was a woman carrying an infant, with a throng of children in tow; she swore they'd all gone to bed hungry the night before. One man approached Ismail asking for financial assistance, whispering yet resolute, as if demanding something he had a right to that had been denied him. And another wanted to be a paid volunteer; he didn't have any skills or qualifications but was willing to do any kind of work for any amount of pay. There was one who dreamed of insulin shots, after having nearly gone blind from diabetes. And there were homeless people, and those who couldn't afford to buy schoolbooks for their children. One man who'd been their neighbor in the American Quarter turned back in embarrassment when he saw Bilal Muhsin's son there, as if he'd come to the wrong place. And there was a paraplegic who took a very long time to say what he wanted. It was an endless sea.

Ismail grew up among them; these were the only people he knew. Their poverty and ailments were an extension of his life and theirs. But when they started coming as destitute beggars, he couldn't take it anymore. He would return home at the end of the day a broken man. He grew more religious and prayed more intensely. In the morning, he would discuss with al-Shami the need to free the *ummah,* the worldwide Muslim community of believers, from the bonds of oppression. Then one day, having grown weary of his daily routine, he remembered Abu Musab. When he asked about him over at the center, one of the guys whispered in his ear that Abu Musab would get in touch with him. That was how things worked with the "ghost" of the association. Much was said about him, but few ever saw him. The little scraps that circulated created a sort of halo around him. He'd met Ayman al-Zawahiri and trained in Afghanistan. Ismail pictured him in many different ways, but what he saw when he finally met the renowned Abu Musab was the last thing he imagined: an ordinary-looking man of medium height wearing worn-out jeans who resembled the bill collector from the electric company who'd quit coming to the American Quarter. He came into the bakery asking for Ismail, so al-Shami escorted them to the back room. That's where their relationship started, amid the sacks of flour and tanks of olive oil. To test his honesty and trustworthiness with money, he sent him to buy some items, knowing ahead of time how much they cost. He liked the fact that Ismail didn't put his nose where it didn't belong, and did what he was told without asking questions. And so he decided to train him for "complex operations." He rented him a motor scooter, and the Sunday before the planned bombing attempt on the Hindu Temple he told Ismail to ride the scooter in the pouring rain toward the capital and scout out where the Sri Lankan laborers and maids gathered to pray. He told him to stop nearby pretending there was something wrong with the scooter, observe their activities, and report back with details. He succeeded in his mission and without realizing what kind of operation he was involved in, he assisted the perpetrator in placing two counterfeit license plates on the Rapid and in preparing the explosive device.

The day the perpetrator of the Hindu Temple bombing was arrested, Abu Musab, out of fear the young man under arrest would crack under interrogation and identify him or Ismail, suggested that Ismail go out into the battlefield. It would be best to take swift action. Ismail didn't ask anyone's advice, didn't hesitate, just went to war never having fired a weapon in his life, except for a few shots at a massive olive tree on the outskirts of the city to test if his father's revolver still worked after so many years.

He gave his mother the cell phone, kissed her hand, asked for her blessing, and when evening fell the next day, he didn't come home. She waited for him all night, tossing and turning in her bed, unable to sleep. In the morning, she went out looking for him. Al-Mashnouq's wife told her she'd seen him rush back to the house the day before, after everyone had left early in the morning. Maybe he'd forgotten something he needed. They could hear him moving around upstairs quite a bit, moving things and organizing things. He came down the stairs carrying a black bag, greeted them very politely, and left.

He left and didn't come back.

"He'll be back," al-Mashnouq stated authoritatively. The same Mashnouq who sat around all day on his rear end, blabbing his mouth off. She asked all of Ismail's friends about him, begging them for any information they could give her. She went to see the bakery owner, but he denied knowing anything. She was sure he was lying, though, even if he did swear to God and on the Prophet Mohammad. Her husband Bilal tried to get some information or any type of lead from what was left of his former comrades, his war buddies from Bab al-Hadid, but to no avail. They complained about not knowing much anymore about the new generation who were being conscripted into jihad over the internet. Ismail's youngest brother heard some talk over at the mechanic garage. He was lying on his back underneath a car, handing his boss various screwdrivers and wrenches as he needed them, when his boss quietly asked him if there was any truth to the rumors that his brother "seeped out." Locals used that water term to refer to young men who had rushed off to faraway places, obeying the edicts of the sheikhs at the mosques or on websites online that stated their home country was the land of *nusra*, of "assistance," not the land of jihad, which meant it was their destiny to travel to offer their assistance. Their heroic deeds would find their way back home to the ears of young boys still too young to enlist. Whether real, fabricated, or embellished, these stories would come from Fallujah or Kandahar or even from Chechnya. These young men would come of age in the world of jihad, having disappeared from view. They took new names, like *Abu Hafs al-Shami*, "the Damascene," or *Abu Obayda al-Shimali*, "the Northerner," and snuck into Gaza through tunnels for transporting provisions and contraband weapons from Al-Arish. Sometimes they'd be killed in a raid by an American drone while carrying out training exercises in Pakistan, in one of the military camps in North Waziristan. In the Anbar Province in western Iraq, they'd plant roadside explosives to hit American Hummers, or maybe their news would disappear, and all memory of them would disappear, too, inside a Syrian prison where they got a good taste of torture in its various forms after being ratted out by some unknown source.

In Ismail's case, Abu Musab immediately put him in the hands of a much older and more experienced mentor. They stayed at a mosque on the outskirts of the city, sleeping for two hours at most, before waking for the dawn prayers. Afterward, the mentor gave Ismail half an hour to read the Quran in his corner. Ismail nearly nodded off before the mentor took the Quran and his ID card from him. He turned over everything he had in his pockets—including a picture of his handicapped younger brother wearing red glasses—and received a fake Iraqi ID in return. They climbed into an old Mercedes, and a second old Mercedes with only the driver inside drove ahead of them. If he ran into a surprise checkpoint along the way, he would turn back quickly and flash his lights to warn them.

They headed up into the mountains, passing through some small Christian villages still sleeping beneath a blanket of morning fog. At the entrances there were billboards advertising concerts hosted by "the Magical Singer" of Aleppo and the dazzling dancer Nour al-Ayn. When they drove past the Cedar Forest, Ismail was surprised by how few trees there were. He used to gaze for hours at those high mountains from his bedroom window in his grandfather's house. They went higher and higher up the mountains, and when he saw some snow he wanted to get out of the car and touch it with his hands, but that was too trivial a matter compared with the serious mission at hand. Before that he'd only known the little pellets of hail the neighborhood kids would catch in the palms of their hands and let melt in their mouths. They also saw some young women wearing colorful ski clothes and dark sunglasses, and a man leading two donkeys laden with firewood. After about an hour and a half, the Bekaa Valley appeared before them like a vast painting in green and yellow. The sun was strong and high now, and Ismail fought his desire to sleep until they took an unexpected turn off the main road. A huge export truck was waiting for them. They got out of the Mercedes without saying goodbye to the driver, who called the mentor "Brother" for the first and last time as he hugged him goodbye.

Without meeting the new driver, Ismail got into the back of the truck and his mentor quickly closed the door shut, drowning him in a darkness he thought he would adjust to once a ray of light found its way in through a crack, but his pupils dilated in vain while the truck heaved around the bends. He remained in total darkness; it was unlike anything he'd ever experienced before in his life. He sat on the floor and tried to get hold of himself by repeatedly hitting his head against the metal, until he got tired and surrendered to the tranquil darkness. He caught a whiff of rotting vegetables and heard the faint sound of some movement and sighing coming from a corner. He sensed the presence of a dog there in the truck, so he kept himself on guard. He was surprised by the sound of someone speaking. The consonants were familiar but the words were obscure, spoken in a heavy accent.

"What?" Ismail asked out into the darkness.

"He's telling you to try to sleep," said a new voice in an easy accent, explaining to Ismail what the other one had said.

"What's that smell?"

"You'll get used to it," the comprehensible voice answered and then added, "Keep drinking water, even if you're not thirsty."

Then he heard a hacking cough and the sound of someone spitting. The time had come to ask the question. "Who's there?"

The familiar voice answered saying the man who had advised him to sleep was a brother from Algeria. "We don't understand him well. We're from the East," he said. There was also a Somali brother accompanying them on their journey who didn't speak at all. "He just coughs and spits."

The truck slowed down before coming to a stop. They could hear the driver answering the border security officer, telling him the truck was headed for Iraq. The officer asked him to bring him a kilo of Ajami tobacco and two boxes of dates on the way back.

"Ask for me, and if I'm not on duty, then write my name on the package and leave it in the customs office. Don't forget."

On the road to Damascus, the truck swerved around a sharp corner and the bags of potatoes fell on top of the men. It started to heat up inside the truck. The man who spoke Arabic with a Berber accent started chanting Surat al-Anfal at the top of his lungs, as if he were in a minaret sounding the call to prayer. But he soon stopped, succumbing to his fatigue. They heard someone's stomach growling, but couldn't tell whose it was. The smell of body odor mingled with that of rotting vegetables. After several hours, the truck came to a stop. They heard the door crack open, and in poured the light of day, along with a voice warning them not to come out suddenly, because the strong sunlight would hurt their eyes.

There were four of them. They got out of the truck into the middle of the desert—four slender shadows. Ismail discovered them for the first time as they looked around in all directions. No one said a single word. They looked at each other and then started moving all at once, though no one planned it. Each walked in a different direction, separating into the open landscape. Once they reached a distance they felt was far enough to hide themselves from one another, they squatted down and relieved themselves for a good, long time. They emptied out everything that was inside them, wiped their bottoms with the hot sand, and traced their steps back to the starting point.

The driver of the truck, in his kufiyah and big black sunglasses hiding his face, was sitting behind his steering wheel waiting for them. They drank hot water from bottles they had to grope around for in the back of the truck after they'd gotten tossed all over the place. They stopped at more borders, passed through more customs, and paid more bribes. And in more deserts, they took care of their bodily needs with the same engineered precision as before, scattering themselves in the four cardinal directions. They suffered the throes of death in that sweltering tomb of a truck bed on one especially long leg of the trip without stops.

Before arriving, Ismail developed a sudden fever. He trembled with chills and his teeth chattered inside that iron oven. He was overcome with a strong feeling that he was disappearing amid the stark darkness. An indomitable force pushed him down. He couldn't see anything, couldn't see himself. He clasped his hands together, patted his head, slapped his palm against his chest to make a sound. His temperature spiked higher, and he started shouting deliriously, repeating his full name as if calling for himself from a deep abyss he was falling into where no one could hear him. He wasn't calling for help, but rather speaking in a tone more like a court bailiff summoning the litigants and witnesses by name in a loud voice despite the fact they're standing right next to him.

"Ismail Bilal Muhsin of the American Quarter!"

He waits for the slightly rolling echo and then adds from time to time, as if reading his ID card, "Mother's name: Intisar al-Omar."

He waits and repeats and goes on about his mother being a maid for the al-Azzam family and about Abdelkarim Bey pruning miniature trees while musing about his ballerina, until the young man whose accent he can understand comes over to help him and tries to lessen his delirium in that dark place. But the moment his journey companion and guide reaches over to touch him, Ismail recoils, bumping his elbow against the metal wall. His companion persists and tries to wrap his arms around him and hold his hands down. He hugs him around the waist rather than the shoulders, which, if the back of the truck were to suddenly be lit up at that moment, would make for a very odd scene: two young men locked together in a strange embrace. He tells Ismail to breathe slowly, and Ismail begins to calm down, knowing at least that someone has heard him, that he's still there, traveling on the journey of his life. He changes his tone and, having awakened halfway, says that this was not where he wanted to die, but rather in jihad in the service of God and the *ummah* of Islam.

He calmed down a bit, and by the time the truck made its final stop, Ismail had forgotten all his prattling inside the back of the truck. The doors were opened, letting in the light, and out they came into the humid, spacious vegetable depot near Mosul. They couldn't stand up for long. They flung themselves, with their stinking bodies that smelled a lot like grilled meat, flat on their stomachs onto the hills of cucumbers and eggplants the vegetable merchants had piled up there before sending them off to market with distributors. Someone came along to spray water on the vegetables, which gave the men a moment to enjoy the sweetness of being alive. They slept for hours, dead to the world, until their new guide came to wake them up and send them off on various missions all over Iraq.

The short one they named "Abu Abdallah al-Somali" without consulting him, the same one who came down with a terrible cough in the back of the truck due to an allergic reaction to the smell of rotting vegetables, originally set out from Mauritania. He traveled by land to Mali, then on to Benghazi, and from there got on a cargo ship carrying livestock and arrived in Latakia. From there he was smuggled across the border with a group of low-wage laborers into Lebanon. After that he smuggled himself back across the borders into Syria and from there to Iraq. He traversed 5,467 kilometers by land and by sea, ready at any moment to meet his maker. Indeed, he longed for that and waited for it. He slept, kept quiet, and waited. He read his Quran in an unintelligible voice. He was dark-skinned and scrawny and had a wart right below his right eye. One spring day, he took off suddenly on a motorcycle and drove into the middle of a big wedding celebration put on by Faylee Kurds in the village of Touzarkoun, in northern Iraq near Khanaqin. He kept going until he reached the middle of the circle of dancers, and there he detonated the explosive vest he was wearing, right into that jubilant mountain panorama beneath a clear blue sky. Not a trace of him remained except for the handlebars of his motorcycle, which got lodged in the trunk of a willow tree a hundred meters away. This Abu Abdallah al-Somali managed to annihilate that massive crowd of native inhabitants of the village of Touzarkoun, whose history as a continuously inhabited place stretched back more than four thousand years, according to archeological experts the government brought in at a time when it was trying to gain favor with the troublesome Kurds. None of the bridal couple's family members survived except a senile grandmother who'd refused to come to her granddaughter's wedding because she wanted to celebrate her own wedding first. The dance troupe was completely wiped out, along with the entire traditional music ensemble and all their instruments—all five dancers, the *mijwiz* player, the *nayy* player, the *taas* player, the *balaban* player, and the tambourine player—none survived except the *tanbur* player who'd gone to relieve himself behind the trees a short distance away only a few minutes beforehand. And if he hadn't had to spend several minutes, like every time, untying his baggy *serwal* trousers and rewinding the red turban that fell off his head while he was urinating, he wouldn't have been spared either. A piece of the *tabla* drum landed on him where he was, as did a woman's shoe—the left, and bits of wood and metal debris fell all around. When he was finally able to get back on his feet and return to the dance area, that Faylee Kurd of medium build was convinced that he had been transported to the Day of Resurrection; he didn't dare ask himself why his was the only body still intact.

The Maghrebi guy with the sharp accent and temperament, the one with the dark spot on his forehead from praying, found his way to the land of *nusra* in Lebanon, via an ordinary Air Algérie Airlines flight. He received intensive training at the Palestinian refugee camp of Ayn al-Hilweh in the south in Sidon, before choosing to fight "in the arena" as they called it. They sent him as backup to Fallujah, which the U.S. Marines were holding under siege. But whether due to faulty instructions or because the road map confused the driver, whatever the case, the car carrying him and other jihadi fighters along with all their weapons, ran into a checkpoint set up on the highway by the Spanish battalion. They exchanged fire, and according to the sole survivor who escaped on foot, the Algerian "brother" put up a valiant fight. He fired his weapon standing in the middle of the road, unshielded, while cursing the Spaniards with the vilest expletives, which were incomprehensible apart from something about their "whore" sisters and mothers. He was able to "incur some harm in their ranks," which is a convenient formula for saying he didn't cause them any serious damage. Up until the soldier Manuel, who'd been stationed in the lookout tower, and who was completing his final tour of duty before retiring and returning to Valladolid, the town of his birth, got nervous and strafed him with his MG3 heavy machine gun that had been upgraded in Turkey specially for use by the Spanish infantry, emptying half the belt, which held more than 200 rounds of ammunition. He cut him in half, down to the waist, killing him while his voice rang out into the suburbs of Fallujah with that Shawia dialect of his that he'd carried with him from his little village in the Aurés Mountains. His mother wrote a letter to the Lebanese Minister of Interior asking about her innocent son who'd been a happy boy that loved life and was full of zest but had been lured in by the cursed internet. They knew he was in Lebanon, but that was the last they'd heard of him. The mother did not receive a reply.

Hatem, the travel companion with the familiar accent, the "Easterner" who comforted Ismail and offered him advice during the trip, got arrested while sleeping in the basement of a building in Baghdad. He never got to experience the jihad he was holding out for, except in the interrogation room at Abu Ghraib prison where the interrogators emptied him of everything he knew. Then they transferred him from solitary confinement to a communal hall where a bearded man wearing a white ankle-length *qumbaz* coat came up beside him and showed an interest in introducing himself. In the evening, others were quick to whisper to him that the nosy fellow was an American informant whose job it was to confirm whether those under suspicion were telling the truth or lying about their identities. After the Nakba of 1948, the grandfather of said Hatem Muhammad Abu Laban left his village in Galilee and took refuge in one of the camps in Jenin, where his father came into this world. From there the family migrated to Jordan after the June 1967 defeat, and three years later, due to his father's zeal for fighting the Jordanian Army with the Democratic Front for the Liberation of Palestine, they left for Yarmouk refugee camp in Damascus. Then he married a Palestinian woman living in Lebanon and moved with her to Shatila refugee camp in Lebanon where, by a miracle, they survived the infamous massacre that took place there. They had eight children together. Hatem was number four, lost somewhere between the older ones whom the parents depended upon to go out and work, and the little ones needing to be looked after at home. Hatem got lost in the middle. He joined the Hamas Youth Brigade and then later a group called "*Jund al-Sham*," Soldiers of the Levant, with comrades who boasted that soon theirs would be the pictures posted on the walls of the refugee camp as "martyrs."

The Americans repeated their interrogation of him one last time, demanding for him to describe how he'd been enlisted, how he'd traveled. They asked once, twice, three times. Details, all the details. The ordinary and the mundane. They demanded to know the names of his associates, but he swore he only knew their nicknames, which were neither here nor there. They asked him to identify pictures. The only one he recognized was Abu Abdallah al-Somali, from a video they showed of him saying he was responsible for the suicide bombing on Touzarkoun. While being interrogated yet again, maybe for the twentieth time, he was in the middle of retelling the story of his voyage to Iraq and the intense heat in the back of the truck, when he suddenly stopped talking. It was as though he'd remembered something, but didn't want to say what. The interrogator, who was an expert, noticed this and accused him of hiding something. Stammering, Hatem denied it, until finally he gave in, stipulating he would give them the name of a brother if only they would put an end to the interrogation. Believing that Ismail had been martyred somewhere and that no harm would come to him, and also confident that their operation would not be exposed, Hatem described in full detail Ismail's ravings in the back of the truck and how he kept repeating his full name, and his place of birth, his address, and even his ID number. He told them everything Ismail had said about his mother, where she worked, about his father's lack of employment, and his crazy uncle the schoolteacher. He told the American interrogator everything, who in turn fed the information into his computer and checked it against the central data bank in Virginia, but found nothing. And so, the two interrogators opened a new file and added it to the database of information on members of terrorist networks:

Name: Ismail Bilal Muhsin
Birthplace: Tripoli, American Quarter, Lebanon
Mother's Name: Intisar al-Omar
Charge: Organized Terrorist Activity

Abu Musab chose young men for jihad from within the Islamic Guidance Association for another group called *"Jund al-Sahaba,"* Soldiers of Companions of the Prophet. And Ismail Muhsin was the least prepared among his comrades on the journey in the back of the truck between Lebanon, Syria, and Iraq. The group's leadership needed to step up operations in its fierce war on "those apostates devising conspiracies and plans to annihilate Muslims." Jund al-Sahaba had them in their sights. "We will not leave a single one of them standing! They will be stricken with every woe imaginable. Our swords can reach deep into their lands, with the permission of God Almighty." And so the choice fell upon Ismail to put this "War into the Depths," into action, and the decision was made to send him south. He was eager to receive orders, even though those in charge of getting him ready didn't seem to think it was important to explain to him the goals of the mission he'd been assigned to carry out. They were in a rush to get someone with connections to the American Quarter. He, too, would be traced back to the American Quarter via the video he recorded during which his mujahideen brothers forbade him from sending a greeting or prayer to his mother. They told him just to identify himself as "Abu Bilal" and his comrades would easily recognize who he was. He memorized the declaration by heart, starting with this Quranic verse as a prelude: *"So the last remnant of the people who did evil was cut off. Praise belongs to God the Lord of all Being."*

They drove him to Baghdad along a route he couldn't possibly remember, stopping on a street that showed signs of affluence. They escorted him to a two-story building, into a room that they locked from the outside. They told him not to leave. The room was equipped with everything he needed: a bathroom, canned food, a television, recordings of heroic suicide missions, and Quranic recitations. Every day he received a visit from a "brother" who asked what he needed and also gave him instructions about the explosive vest—what it was made of and how it worked, and warned him not to set it off by mistake. He threw away his fake Iraqi ID card, which left him feeling completely naked and vulnerable. He handwrote this verse from the Quran:

> *"Every soul shall taste of death; you shall surely be paid in full your wages on the Day of Resurrection. Whosoever is removed from the Fire and admitted to Paradise, shall win the triumph. The present life is but the joy of delusion."*

He shoved it into his pocket, the way his grandmother Imm Mahmoud taught him once after making a space for him to sit down beside her on the old velvet sofa. Then one morning at dawn, the man came into Ismail's room and told him to get undressed. He began fastening the vest on him with great care, wrapping it around his bare waist. He could feel the cold metal pieces against his skin, and how his body and the explosives had become unified, one mass...

He guided him to a bus station for travelers headed south from the capital, and advised him not to board the bus until just before it was about to take off. He told him not to not stop praying in his heart for one second. He stressed the importance of not letting himself stop praying; to silently recite the Sura of Aal-Imran in its entirety and not let anything distract him from praying until he achieved his goal.

"Keep praying, keep praying," the man repeated, over and over again, until he left, and Ismail was on his own.

Ismail chose a big orange bus which was laden with suitcases and other bags. The windows were cloaked in dust from the desert, making it impossible to see the passengers inside. He sat in the last seat as instructed, with the vest of metal screws strapped around his body facing to the front, leaving only those seated behind him to survive the explosion. The passengers were calm. Mostly families—kids and adults.

The bus set out slowly. Ismail had a lapse in his praying, momentarily occupied with the vest united with his body. He tried to lean his head back and shut his eyes, but he didn't last in his darkness for more than a few seconds before another darkness imposed itself, nearly killing him. He tried again and again to no avail— shutting his eyes put him on a precipice he couldn't bear. So, he looked instead at the only scenery available to him out the driver's window where the windshield wipers had carved out two clean semicircles through which one could see the palm trees, the American military vehicles, and the miserable, pallid horizon. He kept his hands away from his body and the explosives, and bowed his head down, keeping his eyes peeled to the floor of the bus. He tried everything to avoid looking at anything else, not even the passenger wearing the white *jalabiya* seated to his left. He didn't get a look at his face, only heard him warning whoever wanted to listen of a sandstorm on the way. He didn't shut his eyes exactly, just pushed one eyelid against the other, letting some light creep in between them. All he could see of what was around him and in front of him were ghosts and splotches of color. He stayed inside his bubble, not allowing his weakness to seep in and undermine his determination. But just before they reached the city of Mahmudiya, where they had instructed him to detonate his vest just as the bus was pulling into the usually crowded station, a little boy appeared in front of him. He remembered what one of his "brothers" had said once about the final minutes being the most difficult. He remembered he should pray to rescue himself. He began with the verse:

> *"And that He might also know the hypocrites*
> *when it was said of them, 'Come now, fight in the*
> *way of God, or repel!' They said, 'If only we knew*
> *how to fight, we would follow you.'"*

He recited the verse, vying with the little boy coming toward him from the front of the bus. He was making his way down the aisle between the seats, one shoe off and one shoe on, just like his younger brother. Ismail looked at him, saw him clearly and completely, walking down the aisle and practicing his numbers by counting the passengers on the bus. He counted each passenger with a tap of his index finger before continuing on his way toward the back of the bus, toward Ismail. Eventually he would come right up to Ismail, face to face with him, and tap him with his finger.

Ismail stopped praying. His whispering ceased. His breathing grew difficult. The boy wouldn't be able to count him without touching him. Ismail might be the last passenger in his computation. When the boy got close to him, Ismail spontaneously put his thumb to his nose and made the comical gesture with his fingers that always made his little brother laugh. Ismail wanted to see the boy's teeth, wanted to make sure he didn't look like his little brother, that he wasn't his brother. When the boy smiled, revealing his missing teeth, Ismail was struck with a sudden bout of vertigo, a tightening in his throat; he was choking. When the little boy reached him and poked him in the chest—on the side where his heart was, with his index finger, counting him as number "thirty-seven," in his strange drawled accent, Ismail relaxed. He was overcome with a strong desire to hug the boy in his arms, ask him his name, kiss him for a long time on his slender neck, if not for fear of accidentally setting off his explosive vest.

At that moment, Ismail's body disengaged from the vest. From deep inside himself, he'd awakened. He could feel the parts of his body moving on their own, independently.

"Muhammad!" cried the boy's mother. He'd gotten very far away from their seats in the second row behind the bus driver.

"Come on. We're here."

Ismail got off the bus at Mahmudiya station. He descended calmly and cautiously. He sucked in his stomach as he walked to keep it away from the vest as much as possible, creating a space between his body and the nails…

He went into the bathroom, removed the belt, and urinated. As he released the liquid from his body, he peered out a small, square window behind the toilet onto a vast horizon that stretched out before him—a landscape void of people, a gradation of colors climbing from the desert to the sky. He urinated for a long time, the longest he could remember of his entire life. He picked himself up and went outside. He took a deep breath and tossed the vest behind the wall of toilets, into a space no one would likely reach anytime soon. He went back and stood there, calm and carefree, amid the crowd of travelers who'd stopped to use the bathroom. The big orange bus pulled up beside him, headed south again after a short rest stop. Ismail craned his neck hoping maybe to see the boy, but most likely he was asleep in his mother's lap, with his ruddy cheeks, exhausted from the long trip.

6

The news came out one morning that the U.S. military had arrested Saddam Hussein, and so al-Mashnouq surrendered to popular will and kept the television tuned to Al Jazeera.

"Don't change it!" warned his wife, who was accustomed to his constantly flipping through the channels, as she attempted to wrestle the remote control from his grip. He, too, had been shocked by the news. He shrieked when Saddam Hussein first appeared, emerging in surrender from his hole in the ground all tired and weary with that overgrown beard. That couldn't possibly be the president of Iraq. It must be some look-alike they were paying to play the role. However, faced with the bitter reality of the situation, al-Mashnouq was forced to relinquish his treason theory. Whoever had been hiding him was persuaded by some crisp green bills—twenty-five million dollars' worth of them, to be exact. He blabbed, took the money, and that was that.

In the scenes that were broadcast incessantly, over and over again, there was a parade of people that appeared on the right half of the screen: Arab journalists, American Middle East experts, and interpreters panting to catch their breath as they tried to translate their analyses of how the arrest was going to affect events in Iraq and the future of the region—things that al-Mashnouq's children quickly grew bored with, causing them to head out the door. They didn't get very far before a loud cry from their mother sent them running back to the TV. Suddenly, there on the Al Jazeera broadcast appeared the face of Ismail, her neighbor Intisar's oldest son. As they transitioned with, "However, the arrest of Saddam Hussein by the allied forces has not put an end to acts of violence and resistance," the station aired a video recording in which Ismail appears, standing in front of a big rock, a machine gun propped against it and a tree that seems to have grown right out of the same rock. He's wearing a camouflaged military uniform and a bandana wrapped around his forehead with "*La Ilaha Illa Allah—Muhammad Rusool Allah,*" There is no God but God; Muhammad is the messenger of God, written on it. However, all the loud cries and comments that came on the heels of his appearance on the TV screen passed without anyone hearing what the deep, masculine voice was saying. When everyone finally settled down, all they heard was the female reporter saying that the videotape was being rebroadcast from "Al-Jihad Online." And she also added that the operation had yet to be confirmed by a second source. Ismail's picture disappeared from the screen, to be followed by an ad for a line of refrigerators and air conditioners made in Korea. Al-Mashnouq turned the TV off with the remote control his wife was unable to confiscate.

"Why did you turn it off?" she whispered.

"So it won't come on again and his family will see it."

One of his sons laughed derisively. Everyone sitting and standing around the darkened TV looked at each other in bewilderment, until the sound of Intisar's voice rang out from upstairs, asking what all the commotion was about. She didn't get any answer. Her question only made the silence that pervaded the bottom floor even heavier.

"Ismail is dead!" she whispered to herself in a choked voice they could hear from downstairs, because they were waiting attentively for the slightest movement from upstairs. She got her answer immediately from al-Mashnouq, who'd gotten past his wife's attempts to stop him from speaking.

"Don't worry. They said the operation hadn't been confirmed yet!"

Al-Mashnouq felt he owed Intisar a bit of reassurance after having been reckless swearing to her the day her son disappeared that he would surely be back after a night or two away from home. A few moments after his hasty reply, the sound of a thud came from upstairs. Sounds from the upper floor always reached the Mashnouq family's ears—footsteps, Bilal's shoes, the dragging of children's feet, or the flushing of the toilet and the long gurgle of water that followed. This thudding sound was heavy and solid. Intisar's little daughter immediately started to cry, and as was usually the case when other people got upset, her handicapped brother let out his long, unrestrained laugh. Al-Mashnouq poked his wife's belly with his elbow and made a gesture with his eyes toward the ceiling. She jumped up and ran upstairs. Her fat legs were still visible from below when she yelled for help.

They lifted Intisar up onto the bed. Al-Mashnouq's wife sprinkled some water on Intisar's face and rubbed her hands while saying a prayer. The moment she opened her eyes, Intisar started asking for her other children, until the little one came and lay down beside her on the bed. The young brother played along, too, and jumped on the bed, landing on top of the two of them. They lifted him off them and covered Intisar and her little daughter with a blanket. She pulled the blanket up over her head, panting and asking for her other son as well. That son, the last she had left, was growing up quickly. She wanted him now.

"Please, bring him to me. Do me this favor."

Al-Mashnouq's son went out to look for him. "Your mother wants you," he told him, though he barely paid any attention. He was standing on the steps with a group of teenagers, with his arms crossed, busy deliberating in a hushed voice with buddies his own age. They would fill the whole neighborhood with news of Ismail's deed. As soon as it got dark, they'd write his name up above the amateur murals—the sea with some palm trees, a huge cascade of fake red roses dangling from an unadorned balcony, a faithful imitation of Caravaggio's *Basket of Fruit* filled with grapes and figs and pears (above which was an ad for an apartment for sale with leasing details and phone numbers, why it was there, no one knew). Exercises in bright still life paintings were what the volunteer artists from the "Achieving Peace Together" organization had chosen one day to liven up the American Quarter. They would write Ismail's name in bold letters, and maybe hang an enlarged picture of him. They all pitched in to pay for a new can of black spray paint, which they would use up completely. They chose the best "calligrapher" among them to spend the night with two "watchmen" while he wrote the heroic martyr Ismail Muhsin's name—"*We are all Ismail Muhsin!*" "*You are in the Garden of Eternity, Ismail!*"— starting from al-Mashnouq's house and all the way to the wheat market on the highway. And they'd tear strips of black cloth and leave them here and there. One of them volunteered to sneak into the Crusader Castle around midnight and hang a flag on its high wall in honor of Ismail. Everyone would see it from the quarter the next morning before the army unit stationed there noticed it.

A little while later, Bilal Muhsin arrived. The news found its way to him at his loitering post on the sidewalk, hitting him like a slap in the face. He got hold of himself and started walking. The house was full of people. He went into the bathroom and sat on the floor. He held his head in his hands and wept bitterly. He cursed himself for having taken Ismail to the train station to show him where he'd carried out his heroic deed, and for having given him his gun, and for applauding him the day he stopped him from beating Intisar. Ismail resembled him—his build, his eyes, his gait. People liked to tease, saying Ismail's only defect was that Bilal Muhsin was his father. So be it.

Bilal sat on the wet bathroom floor a long time. They got worried and opened the door, which couldn't be locked from inside. They brought him out. He was sniffling and sobbing, choking on the tears that had poured from eyes and tear ducts that had for so many years been dry as a bone. He stood there in the middle of the crowded room, in complete submission, with a big round urine stain on the seat of his pants.

But after a little while, a feeling resembling pride crept into Bilal's heart. He pulled himself together and asked more than once to hear the details. They told him about the name Ismail had given himself, "Abu Bilal," which filled him with joy. He'd taken Bilal's name. It was al-Mashnouq who stood there, telling him, with a black bandana wrapped around his head and fire in his eyes as he recited a verse from the Holy Quran. Bilal closed his eyes, imagining his son's final moments. Someone had come to Bilal's rescue in Bab al-Hadid, but no one had come to save Ismail. Bilal's heart ached, but he would stand up and defend Ismail who died instead of him in Iraq. He listened to the young sheikh recently returned from Pakistan who'd brought an uninvited companion along to the house whose guidance and wisdom he assumed they also needed.

"Ismail is in Paradise. Martyrs are next in rank only to prophets and the righteous. Do not weep for him…" He then went on to enumerate the types of martyrs, of which there were seven according to a hadith of the Prophet. In addition to those who die in the divine service of God, those who are stricken with plagues are martyrs, and those who drown, and those stricken with gastric ailments, or pleurisy, and those who die beneath the wreckage…He was interrupted by Intisar's brother Mahmoud who'd come over in a hurry with a group of his friends and told everyone to leave. All the distant acquaintances and passersby who'd been drawn in by all the shouting left the house. Things quieted down a little and Intisar remembered that the day before, her son had tried to call her several times. She clung to what she'd heard, that maybe the news wasn't true. But she didn't move. Her voice came out from under the blanket. "When did it happen?"

"Yesterday…Sit up. Breathe! Why are you burying yourself under there?"

Intisar shrugged her shoulders under the covers to express her opposition.

"The woman is going to die!" cried the wife of Abdelrahman al-Mashnouq, who'd repositioned himself in front of the TV. He kept eyeing the darkened screen every so often, which had been turned off out of respect for Intisar. Al-Mashnouq knew his wife would insist on keeping it that way all day long. He'd have to persevere through the period of silence prohibiting all movement upstairs and downstairs until around midnight when he could make due with a half-hour of wrestling, with the sound muted, until, feeling sleepy, he'd wrap himself in a wool blanket, stretch out on the couch with his head propped on the wooden armrest, and surrender to a deep sleep.

The only thing that would interrupt it when morning came around would be the sound of heavy knocking that would wake him from a dream in which he was on the verge of jumping off the top of the Crusader Castle to float in the air over the river like a paper kite whose string had been cut.

The sound of someone's heavy hand knocking repeatedly on the front door was followed by the sound of someone shouting with the intent to instill fear. "Mukhabarat!" It was the voice of that sergeant with the moustache and the broad shoulders.

The whole quarter was familiar with the morning patrol. The sound of military boots pounding against the stone steps, and the cocking of rifles with the occasional final command to fire them if a detainee made an attempt to flee or if a young man picked up his pace when noticing a patrol spreading out in the neighborhood.

One could see in their eyes that the neighborhood folk resented it in their hearts. Although they brought their sons regular income and health insurance, it was like being born with the "government's gun" aimed at their heads. "She gets pregnant in Sweden and gives birth here!" they'd complain, after reading in the newspapers about "a crackdown on a band of Islamic fundamentalists and the confiscation of a cache of explosives in a Paris suburb. Investigations uncover ties to Peshawar and to Lebanon." Ties to Lebanon meant here, their neighborhood.

Busybodies flocked around al-Mashnouq's house. They peered out their windows and from their balconies, came out in their pajamas to see what was going on. Men patrolled the area in every direction with their weapons drawn, as if an enemy combatant was lurking around the next corner ready to jump out at them at any moment. And there was another face looking down at them—the picture of the soccer player, the captain of the Ta'adud Club who'd been killed a few days earlier in a shooting incident in which his best friend accidentally shot him in the heart. A huge picture of him had been posted there on a nearby wall, with a prayer written beneath it: "*Oh God, I have suffered an injustice, help me!*"

Al-Mashnouq opened the doors, rubbing his eyes.

"Get dressed and come outside! All of you—young and old!" shouted the sergeant. "And bring your IDs!" he added.

Out they came, one after the other. The entire al-Mashnouq family. Half asleep, annoyed. The first to come down from upstairs was Bilal. A new man, his black eyes sparkling, he stood firmly with his head held high and his shoulders back, as if he owned the place.

"What do you want?" he said, with his hands resting on both sides of the double door. "This is the house of Ismail Bilal al-Muhsin," he said firmly, adding the definite article "al-" to his family name.

"*Allahu Akbar!*" cried one of the young men of the quarter. Some other voices repeated it after him.

Someone in the back of the crowd pushed Ahmad, nicknamed "Love"—the quarter's idiot—forward, opening a path for him as if sending him on an urgent mission. When "Love" reached the sergeant with the handlebar moustache, he flashed that legendary smile of his and hastily put his hand out, begging for alms.

"Get him away!" shouted the officer, intending Bilal, but the sergeant shoved "Love" with his heavy hand instead. The poor beggar went reeling and nearly fell to the ground as he cowered away like a dejected dog.

"What shame!" shouted a woman holding a baby in her arms from her balcony. Other cries of disapproval rose up around the quarter.

Meanwhile, after having awakened the entire household, Intisar remembered Ismail's cell phone. She had to get rid of it. She took it out of her purse and opened the window meaning to throw it behind the house. But just as she was about to throw it, she realized the phone was the only link she had to her son, and so she hid it behind the toilet seat. Then she took her handicapped son by one hand and her other son by the other and went downstairs. She was going to hold onto her second son's hand the whole day long, and she promised herself she would never let him go. She would never leave the house after that day, wouldn't go to the Azzam house; she would keep tabs on him. At night, he had snuck out to meet up with his buddies as they had planned. Some sort of intuition caused her to wake up and notice something missing from the next bedroom. She got down on her knees and started groping in the pitch dark, checking for her children. He wasn't there. When he came back home at the crack of dawn, after writing all over the walls of the quarter with his buddies, she couldn't bring herself to scold him. Instead she went and lay down beside him. He woke up in the morning to the sound of the Mukhabarat's shouting and knocking at the door. He stood up. She stood up next to him. He let her hold his hand as they came downstairs together to find two soldiers trying in vain to move Bilal away from the front door. Some strange force had inhabited his skinny body. They teamed up on him as ordered by the officer and scooped him up in one go. They lifted him by the torso and his body disappeared inside their green military uniforms. He gave up resisting with his arms and his legs and focused what strength he had left on his neck and shoulders. They carried him out amid the rising clamor of protest. He had surrendered all of himself except his head, which he held high, and his dark, piercing eyes that glimmered with intensity as he looked around in every direction so that no native son of the American Quarter would miss seeing the vengeance of Bilal Muhsin—upon a past that had beaten him down so forcefully up until the day before.

When they carried him past the commanding officer, he shouted in a more modified tone this time, "To the truck!"

They carried him down to the area near the river where they had parked their vehicles. They looked like a winning team carrying their champion teammate on their shoulders.

They separated the children from the adults amid the repeated shouts from the sergeant warning the children to be quiet. A young man wearing glasses and carrying a briefcase entered the house. He went through both floors searching for evidence. He bent down to look under the benches in the patio area outside, he looked behind the television, went upstairs to the second floor, looked out the only window up there. Sometimes people resorted to hanging things they wanted to hide outside windows. He soon arrived at the bathroom and found the mobile phone. He checked the phone's memory and discovered that no outgoing calls had been made but many calls, all from the same number, had come in. He finished his inspection through the two stories of the house and turned the booty over to the officer who raised the red Nokia 8890 in the air and asked, "Who does this phone belong to?"

Intisar's heart went wild again.

No one answered.

Silence prevailed. All eyes were on the officer as he pulled his own cell phone out of his jacket pocket. He held it in his right hand and fumbled a little bit having one phone in each hand before figuring out a way to make a call from the confiscated phone. His phone rang amid the public scrutiny and the number appeared on the screen.

He repeated his question, "Who's number is 03-156782?"

His answer came in the form of a woman's voice, rattling off a tirade of random words that reached the officer's ears, just before she appeared on the scene in a rush from the second floor in a daytime hallucination. "Hell…Forbidden…Shame…" were the only ramblings that found their way to people's ears.

Hamideh, the one they also called "the Madwoman." She came down the stairs with the nimbleness of a dancer, slender and draped in her black *niqab* veil. She stood before the soldiers, staring them in the face and spewing curses at them. They were at a loss as to what to do with her, so they just smiled. She finished her little jaunt past them, knowing they wouldn't touch her, took a couple steps down the stairs and turned to look back at them and launch a few more curses—the same ones she would spew again, as she did every day, at the vendors and other customers at the vegetable market while waving that little black purse of hers, with the shiny white metal studs, in their faces.

There was a moment of hesitation during which a voice from the back resumed shouting in the face of the secret police. "*Bi-rruh, bid-damm, nafdika ya shahid!*" With our souls and with our blood we will redeem you, dear martyr! Then came the first stone, which landed on the shoulder of one of the soldiers. He wasn't sure what to do, so he turned to the commanding officer. His fellow soldiers raised their rifles. One of them cocked his. Then a second stone fell and shouting ensued. The officer drew his gun and shot it in the air. The crowd backed away a little. The soldiers pointed their weapons at chest level, and the officer demanded to know who threw the stones. Someone said it was some children who ran off and were too fast to catch. Finally, al-Mashnouq ended the matter, saying, "If you're looking for Ismail Muhsin, he's not here. He was martyred in Iraq. We saw it yesterday on Al-Jazeera."

Intisar squealed in pain as if hearing the news for the first time. The little one wrapped her little arms around as much of her mother's body as she could and buried her head. The neighborhood women wiped the tears from their eyes with handkerchiefs. The officer ordered his men to withdraw, satisfied with his one bit of loot.

News of the Mukhabarat's presence in the neighborhood reached Yasin al-Shami, the baker, sending a sudden pain down his spine as he sat. He didn't usually suffer from that particular pain unless he was walking, which forced him to lean a little to the right as he walked to relieve it. But now the strong pain had taken hold of him. As soon as he started to form a thought, that moment when they'd broken his back would come flooding back into his mind. The pain came in a succession of waves, and along with it came the memory of the horrible smells of the prisons. Each prison they dragged him to had a particular smell in his memory. Never again would he put himself at the mercy of vicious dogs tearing at his flesh. At this point in his life, he deserved death, not torture.

He unlocked the cash box with his key and stood next to it ready to carry out the pact he'd made with himself a long time ago. First, he would unpin the grenade and throw it at whoever came to arrest him. Then he would grab the machine gun he had stashed in the stock room in the back. He would fire the gun in every direction, emptying one magazine and reloading with a second one. A sixty-round shootout to the death.

He construed what was happening outside from his morning customers. It made him very nervous when they told him al-Mashnouq's house was surrounded, and he was relieved to know their search came up empty except for a cell phone, but still he was not at ease. He heard the clamor of their approach before actually seeing them. A soldier appeared in his doorway, with his back toward him. Yasin reached for the grenade and held it in his hand. If the soldier turned to look at him he would pull the clip and throw it at him. But suddenly someone shouted an order that he couldn't quite make out and all the soldiers took off running. None of them turned to look at Yasin. He locked the grenade back inside the drawer and went out to the sidewalk, where he watched the scene unfold: Bilal Muhsin waving back at the children from the truck as they chased after it, shouting for their slain martyr, until the caravan of military vehicles disappeared into the early morning city streets.

They took Bilal into one of the military barracks on the outskirts of the city. They gave him a perfunctory interrogation which opened the gates to a flood of information they didn't ask for. He threatened the Americans, warning they would never take Iraq, because Arab land was sacred, and there were thousands of young men who would follow in Ismail's footsteps. Then, without being asked, he told them all about the Bab al-Hadid rebellion and Sheikh Imad and his war buddies. He recalled names and dates. They got so bored listening to him that they stopped writing it down. They closed the report and told Bilal to sign it. He read it over and when he protested that his last comments were not included in the deposition, they scolded him and told him to leave. He went out of the barracks with a confident stride and headed for the city. He would return to Bab al-Hadid with his head held high. No one was going to accuse him of running away. No one was going to ridicule him.

Bilal walked down the side of the road, watching the passing cars, at nearly the exact same moment that his son Ismail, in the city of Mahmudiya south of Baghdad, was watching the orange bus disappear around a distant bend as he walked away clean. They didn't ask him his name in Mosul or in Baghdad; he wasn't expected anywhere at any certain time. The world was all his. The roads stretched out before him, open and sunny, just like those mornings when he would skip school and wander through the alleys of the American Quarter. He passed a throng of women chirping in a thick and difficult Iraqi accent. One of them, a short, fat woman, was saying things to the others and dishing out smiles and laughter to each one. He looked at them as if he'd never seen women with head scarves and colorful long flowing robes before. The cars came in waves down the wide street. People dressed in their tattered clothes sat on their rooftops, shouting jubilantly. A long procession of cars of every type and model rolled along the street celebrating the capture of the tyrant. "Like a rat they pulled him out of that hole," said a hastily written banner. "Give him death!" yelled the crowd as the dust rose up from beneath the tires, engulfing them and him as he gazed at their joyful faces. One of them threw his sandal up in the air in delight and it landed in front of Ismail. A smile formed on his face, the first smile in many long months.

He didn't have to report to anyone. He had been given a small sum of money, which he used to buy a backpack, a lightweight hat, and some bottled water. He left Mahmudiya on foot, choosing to walk merely for the sake of walking. He liked the scorching sun. His deed had been erased; he'd been cleansed of it and become a mere shadow walking along the side of the road, paying no heed to the busses that beeped at him as they passed, hoping to bring him on board with the other passengers. An American soldier waved to him from his perch atop a sand-colored military vehicle. He sped up his pace, answering the call of a verdant oasis that appeared to his right. He lay on his back amid the high, moist grass. The chirp of a cicada sounded in the air and the deep sound of passing trucks rumbled in the distance. Ismail slept peacefully, swimming in a fragrant abundance of wild yellow daisies. He dreamt a series of childlike dreams, like choice selections of happier days, until the sound of car horns woke him up. A procession of cars was speeding along before having to slow down at the city limits. They were still celebrating the capture of Saddam Hussein. Ismail lay there in the shade for a long time. He felt the need to urinate again and wondered where all that liquid could possibly have come from. He hoisted the backpack onto his shoulders and resumed his trek along the main road. He grew smaller and smaller as he walked into the horizon, eventually transforming into a little black dot hovering over the surface of the mirage created by the new asphalt that laid out for him a road stretching from Mahmudiya to Baghdad.

Baghdad…Hungry, he reached the expansive city at sunset, drawn deeper and deeper into it by some hidden force. He came upon a kiosk selling mobile phones and suddenly remembered his mother and her phone. He still remembered the number; it had been engraved in his memory. His only thread. He bought a cheap used phone and sat down on the curb to call her. When he heard it ringing on the other end, he suddenly felt as if a wall had gone up between him and his other life that his voice wouldn't pass through. He dialed his mother numerous times from many different places. She'd answer and he wouldn't be able to speak. He'd hear her voice and hang up. He was unable to say a single word. All he wanted was to hear her voice and ask about his little disabled brother. He tried to speak but his voice was stuck inside. Likewise, when his new phone suddenly rang the next day, and the voice on the other end of the line said he was Abdelkarim al-Azzam, Ismail failed to get out a single word.

He asked about a hotel where he might spend the night, and they sent him to an inn in the Ghadir neighborhood near

Palestine Street. They made him pay in advance. He was the only lodger until a family of three generations came at dusk—a grandmother, a father, a mother, and some children. They were Christians who had sold everything they owned. They were going to spend the night at the inn before traveling the next day to Syria and from there to Lebanon and then possibly to Canada or Sweden. The grandmother told him their story. She was a fair-skinned woman, still beautiful. She noticed him the moment they entered the little inn, as she said, and could tell he wasn't Iraqi. She wanted to know who he was and what he was doing there. "I'm from Lebanon," said Ismail without thinking.

"And what are you doing in Baghdad?"

The grandmother's question hung in the air there at the inn.

She wasn't going to back off. She told him about some relatives of theirs in Lebanon and mourned the fact that she would die outside Iraq, would not be buried beside her family members. She was going with her son and his family because they refused to leave without her.

"Will you take me with you?"

The question came out of his mouth on its own. Some force greater than himself made him wish for it. Maybe it was the force of his mother and his little brother.

A look of friendliness in his eyes and a simple calculation that the presence of a young Muslim man along with them in the car might ease the emigrant family's burden when going through checkpoints, led the sixty-year-old woman, who held tightly to the Virgin Mary pendant hanging from her neck, to agree to let him accompany them.

And just as the grandmother was informing the family that they would be taking on an extra passenger, he heard himself saying again that just this morning he'd lost his identity papers in Mahmudiya.

Again, she didn't back down. After only a brief hesitation, she found an easy solution.

"You're the same age as my grandson. He went ahead of us to Syria and we have a second ID of his. You can use it when needed." Then she added, smiling, "You look a lot like him anyway."

And just like that, his fate was resolved there in the lobby of that gloomy inn, somewhere between the face of his mother, which hadn't stopped beckoning to him since he got off the bus in Mahmudiya, and the face of this unveiled woman who, in her dress and demeanor resembled those Christian women who used to trail behind the priest to the Church of the Virgin in the American Quarter.

Early the next morning, the family boarded a bus just big enough to accommodate all of them and their suitcases, after having listened the day before to the last sermon of the church priest in which he boasted for the thousandth time that they were the first Christians and were the only ones who spoke the language of Jesus of Nazareth. They crossed into Syria the same day, without being stopped by anyone. On the contrary, the armed guards and regime soldiers waved them through quickly, all except one checkpoint at the Jordanian border where the soldier simply asked for the names of all the passengers, without asking for IDs. The grandmother took it upon herself to introduce everyone, calling Ismail by her grandson's name. They were able to reach Damascus that same evening and spent the night with some relatives who'd gone ahead of them. Ismail insisted on completing the trip to Lebanon the next day and reached the American Quarter that night.

He made a point to arrive at night, by way of the high hill. It was when he passed in front of his uncle's closed shop that he read his name: *"Our Martyr Ismail Muhsin."*

Stricken with vertigo, he panicked like a cat suddenly caught under a spotlight. That wall from before rose up in front of him once again. He tipped his hat down over his face and took a few steps back until he thought he'd escaped the circle he'd plunged into. Then he turned around and walked away, only to see his face in another place right beside him: *"Our martyr has surely won his place in Paradise"*—signed, *"Friends of the Martyr Ismail Muhsin."*

Frightened, he turned and climbed back up the hill with hurried steps. He could hear the voices of two young men. He knew them. He slowed down, hoping they wouldn't notice him. They were not expecting to see Ismail there, so they didn't recognize him. They didn't even look his way. Their voices faded as they made their way down the hill and Ismail took off like lightning, without looking back. The streets were deserted. All the shops were closed. He wandered around for an hour before settling at the rundown grist mill on the riverbank where he used to swim naked with his buddies. As he looked toward the American Quarter with its scattered night lights, he suddenly realized he had left that world a long time ago. His buddies all remained young adolescents while he was left to grow up, all alone, propped against the millstone waiting for morning to come, unable to sleep a wink. He prayed the morning prayers as soon as he heard the *adhan* from the Attar Mosque. He got up, picked an orange from a tree, and as he was peeling it with his fingers, the image of Abdelkarim al-Azzam popped into his mind. He was overcome with a strange feeling of nostalgia he wasn't expecting to feel for the resident of that big house. And so, he pulled himself together and set out for it along a back road.

What he didn't know was that the "Information Cell," as they called it, informed the Mukhabarat that the surveillance on Intisar Muhsin's cell phone had produced the following results: numerous calls were made from an Iraqi phone number to the Lebanese cell phone that had been confiscated from the suspect's home; in addition, numerous calls originating from a Lebanese landline had been made to the same Iraqi phone number; the Lebanese phone number was registered in the name of Abdallah Mustapha al-Azzam. The officer chose to proceed with caution. He dialed the number written there in front of him and hung up as soon as someone picked up on the other end. It was a man's voice. When the CIA report of the investigation of Ismail Muhsin arrived, those in charge at the Information Cell were impressed by the level of detail of the information spelled out by the Americans. According to the report, the suspect was extremely dangerous and belonged to the Iraqi branch of Al-Qaeda called "Al-Qaeda of Mesopotamia." The report went on to say that for unknown reasons he failed to carry out the suicide bombing he'd been sent to do in Iraq—despite the video that had been broadcast on Al Jazeera, as suicide bombers sometimes failed to carry out these attacks. And there was a good chance the suspect had returned to his home country.

An informant in the American Quarter was asked to keep his ears open for any news or talk of Ismail Muhsin and report back. Also, twenty-four-hour surveillance of the Azzam home was set up, according to the officer's orders.

"Inform us of everything that goes on, and no matter what happens, don't make a single move without consulting the administration. Watch out for the sons of noble families. This guy's grandfather was a bigshot!"

He was alluding to Mustapha al-Azzam, of course.

Three agents took turns sitting behind the wheel of the new white Mitsubishi jeep with internal security license plates that was parked on the side of the road outside the Azzam house. Each took an eight-hour shift. They used the restrooms at the pastry shop when necessary, and alternated between shawarma or falafel sandwiches when they got hungry. They got very bored. The first few days people on the streets and local inhabitants thought the four-wheel drive vehicle might belong to some high-ranking officer's body guards, and that maybe the officer had recently moved into one of the new apartments there.

It wasn't long before the three watchmen started commenting to one another about the pretty African maid who worked for one of the noble families in the area. The man on the morning shift caught sight of her coming down the sidewalk, so he flashed his headlights at her, lighting her face up into a smile. When she walked past him, he sent some sweet talk her way. He was busy checking out the way she wiggled her bottom in his rearview mirror when Ismail Muhsin arrived on the scene. Using the wall as cover and with the hat he'd bought in Iraq tipped down over his face, he walked right past the surveillance agent and slipped in to the Azzam residence through the front gate. He climbed up and shimmied himself in through the kitchen window. Completely exhausted, he plopped down onto the couch and immediately fell asleep.

Abdelkarim stood frozen in the doorway when he came down to drink some water and found Ismail sleeping there. Abdelkarim had become a prisoner of sorts the last few days, ever since Intisar stopped coming. The house was a total mess. His dirty laundry had piled up in the kitchen, and at night he slept amid a chaos of sheets and blankets, as if he'd never lived alone before. He ate very little and drank a lot. He saw Ismail curled up on the same couch where his mother had told him to sleep. He thought he was dead. It crossed his mind that maybe they'd brought Ismail's dead body to his house. A few days earlier, Intisar had sent someone to apologize to Abdelkarim and let him know she would not be coming for a whole week because her son had been martyred. "Her son, Ismail. Intisar Muhsin says you know him," said the woman messenger who, when he opened the door, Abdelkarim thought was a beggar.

Seeing Ismail there, with nothing on except his dirty blue jeans and a tattoo of the Angel of Death covering his back, Abdelkarim was at a loss as to what he should do. He called to him quietly, but he didn't hear. He was afraid to touch him and have him roll off dead onto the floor. He called to him a little louder, and Ismail moved. He wasn't dead.

He sat up, apologizing for sneaking in, while putting on his shirt to cover himself and his tattoo.

"I don't want to go home. My mother always says our only recourse is the Azzam family, ever since my grandfather's time. But I promise not to stay long. I'll leave today...or tomorrow."

"Stay here as long as you like. This is your house! Were you in Iraq?"

"I was on a bus in a city they call Mahmudiya. I saw a boy and thought, 'That's my brother,' and I saw a mother and thought, 'That's my mother.'"

Abdelkarim didn't try to understand. "Why did the news report say you were dead?"

"I don't know. Please I just have one request of you. Tell my mother I'm still alive."

Abdelkarim al-Azzam considered the distance to the American Quarter and imagined the route he would take to get there. He feared the city but he would cross it. He wasn't going to leave Ismail to suffer his fate. He concealed himself with a pair of dark sunglasses and headed out the front door. The surveillance agent saw him and recorded the first movement worthy of note during his monotonous mission.

Abdelkarim walked with hurried steps, traversing the distance with ease until he reached the river and noticed a man in the distance with his hands in his pants pockets, leaning over the railing of the iron bridge. No one paused to watch him. The man looked up at the sky and called out in a feeble, monotonous tone, deliriously without stopping or waiting for a response. He looked up to the heavens as if he could see exactly who he was calling to. *"Ya Rahman, Ya Rahim, Ya Alim, Ya Mu'in,"* O Compassionate One, O Merciful One, O All-Knowing One, O Helpful One… He continued to hear the man's voice all the way to the bottom of the steps leading up to the American Quarter. Then, looking up at the Crusader Castle, he remembered. A cannonball had hit its high wall, carving a scar into it like a painful wound.

He made his way all the way up to the house. Al-Mashnouq's wife called out to Intisar in a loud voice and she came running, draped in black, to apologize to him for not coming to clean his house since hearing about Ismail. Al-Mashnouq's wife followed behind them trying to eavesdrop on their conversation, but they walked away from the house.

"Ismail is not dead!" He said it with conviction, and she nearly leapt into his arms to hug him, but instead flung herself at his hand, kissing it as he struggled to pull it away.

"Don't tell anyone! He only wants you to know."

As they stood there beneath a banner with the image of Ismail as he'd appeared on television printed on it, with the caption "Our struggle is but a victory for God most Glorious," she started to tell him how the sheikhs offered to perform the "prayers for the absent one," but she flatly refused because she didn't believe it. She didn't want to. She reached for Abdelkarim's arm, put her hand in his, and went on to tell him she didn't believe it a few days later when al-Mashnouq's son brought her a sum of money he'd been given by a bearded sheikh who'd summoned him from the quarter by name. He'd taken him aside and handed him an envelope. "Deliver it to the martyr's mother in person." She opened the envelope and refused to touch the money. "Take it back to whoever gave it to you. Ismail isn't dead." Intisar was overjoyed, in a state of happiness she'd never experienced before in her entire life. Then, suddenly, she stopped her chatter and, looking up at Abdelkarim as if at her lover, she asked, "Where is he?"

"He wants you to bring him the gun."

"The gun?" she asked, a bit disappointed. "What does he want with the gun?"

"He wants it at any cost. He hid it up on the roof inside a powdered milk tin. His younger brother knows how to climb up there."

He stood waiting for her while Intisar tried to flee the questions al-Mashnouq's wife was whispering behind her back. The woman turned toward Abdelkarim and invited him to honor them with a visit inside the house, but he declined the invitation with an embarrassed smile. He was uncomfortable standing there in front of the people of the quarter as they passed by, clearly taken by his elegance and delicate movements and gestures. They bombarded him with curious glances and all sorts of questions until Intisar finally reappeared, her black purse in hand, beaming with the joy of having gotten Ismail back and the pleasure of plotting secretly with Abdelkarim al-Azzam. They walked down together, eventually disappearing around a corner. Just before they passed in front of the butcher shop, Intisar pulled out a heavy black plastic bag from her purse and handed it to Abdelkarim.

"Be very careful," she warned. "May God protect you."

She wanted to hold his hand again, to touch him, but he stepped back. She headed back to the house, promising herself to make her way to the Azzam house early the next morning. Meanwhile, Abdelkarim looked around cautiously and took the opportunity to tuck the revolver into his belt while no one was watching. He tossed the black plastic bag onto the butcher's waste pile and crossed the iron bridge, returning to the place where he'd seen the delirious man. Abdelkarim slowed his steps as soon as he caught sight of him in the distance. He'd changed his cycle of movements: now he leaned over the river, drew energy from it and then straightened up, standing tall with his arms reaching toward the grey, cloud-filled sky, crying out the names of God. And as before, no one turned to look at him.

Abdelkarim walked with confident steps, checking to feel the gun at his hip from time to time. He was buoyed by the urgency of his task, in a hurry to get home. He entered his house just as he had left it, without noticing the car parked outside across the street. He locked the door behind him and gave the gun to Ismail. He told him that the Mukhabarat had been to the American Quarter looking for him and that he must be extremely cautious and not go out into the streets. And he also added, "Your mother never believed you were dead!"

Abdelkarim went into his bedroom, leaving Ismail suspended amid a feeling that hadn't left him since seeing that picture of himself on the walls of the American Quarter the night before. He couldn't remember when the picture had been taken, but every time that image came into his mind, of his own face, blown up in such large proportions, with his eyes looking directly at him, and right beside the poor captain of the Ta'adud Club soccer team who'd been accidentally killed, he realized he'd reached the end of the road. After the Azzam house, he had no other place to go. The moment he stepped outside, his life would be completely exposed. Even there, he was unable to look Abdelkarim in the eye. He averted his eyes when he spoke to him, embarrassed for himself and for Abdelkarim. He was trapped there inside his mother's kitchen. He felt for his father's gun, held it in his grip as if holding his fate in his hands, ready and willing to do something to himself if necessary. But then his thoughts would return to Intisar, to his little brother, and after an hour of tossing and turning on the kitchen sofa he fell into a deep sleep the likes of which he hadn't tasted except in small, tiresome doses since returning from Iraq.

Ismail dozed off just as Abdelkarim was suffering through a bout of anxiety, bothered by a succession of strong emotions. He had been taken aback when he heard about Intisar's son dying in Iraq. He loved him. He mourned him and felt sorry for the loss of him. He imagined him blowing up and flying into the air in a million pieces. He wept for him. He lamented for Intisar and imagined her face full of sorrow. He envied Ismail for having followed a path that Abdelkarim, yet again, was forever barred from. And then he found him that morning, alive, and he was disappointed by him at first. He'd saved his own skin, like all the rest. But then he was happy because Ismail came back, and specifically there to his house, because life had won out. He was happy for him and happy for Intisar and for that exuberance that poured from her eyes as they descended the steps of the quarter together. He would help him and protect him—the grandson of Imm Mahmoud, the son of Abdallah al-Azzam.

He couldn't sleep. He washed his face several times. He flipped through the stacks of old movie posters his father had gotten for him, through his friend, the owner of the Metropole, as a consolation for not allowing him to go to movie theatres. Then he turned on the television, flipped through all the stations, and then turned it off. He opened Valeria's closet and rummaged through her clothes. He tried to walk on tiptoes like a ballerina. He took one step and fell. Men's toes were not made for such ballet moves, as they called them. He kept trying, though, as he made his way toward his CD collection. He selected *The Barber of Seville*, inserted it into the drive, and turned the volume all the way up. The speakers vibrated with the opening notes of the prelude, waking up several of his neighbors at that early hour before dawn, causing them to peer out from a balcony or window to see what was going on. It also alarmed the security guard behind the steering wheel of his jeep, causing him to turn off his car radio and perk his ears. The task he and the other guards had been assigned had so far been fruitless, so when the music blared from the very house under surveillance, it broke the monotony of the situation. The guard didn't waste any time calling into headquarters to tell them something suspicious was going on inside the house.

Awakened by the loud noise, Ismail judged from how tired he felt that he'd only been asleep for a few minutes. He felt drunk. It took him some time to figure out where he was, after having tried to sleep in so many different places on his journey from the mosque to the dark back of the truck and from the jungle of Mahmudiya to the mill beside the river. He opened the kitchen door that led to the salon and found it all lit up. At first glance he didn't recognize Abdelkarim, but rather figured out gradually, amid the blur of conflicting images, that the person trying to stand on tiptoes and attempting, with great difficulty, to spin himself around only to fail and then switch to trying with his feeble voice to accompany Count Almaviva as he serenaded Rosine at her balcony—was Abdelkarim. Ismail came into the room and sat in the same place he'd been talking to him that night, surrounded now by the chaotic voices in the background while Abdelkarim alternated between singing along and dancing. He'd take one light step, lift his leg into the air, wave his arms in time with the music, do a pirouette, and then go back to the middle of the room to start all over again.

The internal security police arrived in the area. Ismail heard the sirens and jumped up from his chair.

"They're not going to arrest me! I won't turn myself in!"

He ran to the kitchen, grabbed his gun and loaded it. He came back into the salon and took position, his gun aimed toward the front door.

Abdelkarim stopped his silly dance and turned the music off. They could hear military orders being shouted outside. His heart torn up, he screamed at Ismail, "They'll kill you!"

"I'm dead anyway!"

Abdelkarim looked around and then came up with an idea. "No, you're not dead. Wait."

He rushed to Valeria's closet and grabbed a pile of her clothes. He brought them into the salon and spread them out on the furniture, looking through them for the black trench coat she had been wearing the day she appeared to him on the Route 21 bus. Ismail was still shirtless the way he always slept, no matter how cold the weather. Abdelkarim grabbed the coat and put it on him, covering the Angel of Death tattoo on his back. He didn't leave Ismail any choice. He pushed him toward the kitchen door that opened to the back yard.

"Hurry up! Jump out the back!"

"Where will I go?"

He didn't answer. He tied the belt of the baggy coat up around his neck and helped him up onto the fence between two weeping fig trees.

"They won't recognize you. Get away before the sun comes up..."

Then he added, "Return the coat to me if you can someday. It was Valeria's, as you know!"

"I'll be back..."

He hesitated a moment, and then, from on top of the wall

he made a gesture with his fingers indicating the small size of the thing and said, "I'll come back for my little tree…"

Abdelkarim signaled for Ismail to hurry and make his escape and then went back into the salon to listen to Maria Callas with the volume turned up while waiting for the military to come in. He had done all he could do.

They scoffed under their breath at the colorful women's clothes strewn all over the furniture. They searched the rooms, asked about Ismail Muhsin, but they weren't content with mere denial and disavowal. They asked Abdelkarim Al-Azzam to come down to the "Administration Branch" as they called it, where they asked him questions the officer helped him to answer—since, in the meantime, his cousin Riyad had made use of his connections and influence to have the case closed. All that remained, in a desk drawer, was a brief report about surveillance of the Azzam house, which was under suspicion for housing Ismail Muhsin, a suspect in bombing attacks in Iraq and for his participation in the attack on the Hindu temple and for committing a variety of other crimes. However, information from "reliable sources" in the American Quarter all indicated that Ismail had died in Iraq, the result of a suicide bombing. There were posters and banners all over the quarter honoring him. The report went on to say there had been a raid on the Azzam house after the police received a complaint against the suspect, Abdelkarim Al-Azzam, for disturbing the peace with his blaring music during the wee hours of morning. Upon entering, they found the suspect to be intoxicated, too drunk to provide any information. He refuted with resolution, however, having seen Ismail Muhsin, and asserted that Ismail had "died a martyr." They were forced to let him go for lack of evidence, and moreover, it was unlikely he was closely connected to the suspect, considering he was merely the son of the maid.

Intisar—she had come by foot all the way from the American Quarter early in the morning. Of course, the first to notice her had been Abdelrahman al-Mashnouq. She'd come downstairs alone, and since he didn't hear children's footsteps, he didn't switch the TV from the fashion channel with all the models walking up and down the runway in their underwear. He was surprised she wasn't wearing black, even though it had only been a few days since her son's death. And she hadn't gone back to wearing the proper religious attire Ismail had made her wear, but rather had on the pair of tight blue jeans that outlined her figure. She greeted al-Mashnouq, glanced over at his fashion models on the TV, and smiled at him for the first time since they'd become neighbors. She was unbothered by his stare, which was aimed at her bottom, and maybe she even wiggled it just a little as she went out the door and descended the stairs with elegant confidence. She traversed the city streets with a bounce in her step, arriving at the Azzam house only moments after the police left with Abdelkarim in their custody. She had promised herself she was going to see Ismail, so she didn't respond to the provocation of the concierge of the building next door when he told her all about the "songs," as he called them, that had caused all the commotion. She found the front door wide open. She went inside, picked up the ballet clothes and put them away in the closet. When she saw Abdelkarim's neatly made and unslept-in bed, she got worried. But she waited. She waited until sunset, when they released him and all of a sudden, there he was in the doorway. Startled, she ran to him and they held each other in a spontaneous embrace. Abdelkarim felt a powerful surge of desire for her. Wrapping his arms around her and hugging her close to him, he told her Ismail was alright. She closed her eyes and buried her head in his chest. For several minutes they held each other that way, neither one making any effort to be released from the other's embrace.

Intisar resumed her daily housecleaning chores at the "Abdallah Al-Azzam Residence." Her monthly pay, which included a raise, was always there on the kitchen table at the end of the month. She shooed the beggars and busybodies away, polished the chandeliers with extra care once a month, aired out Valeria's clothes, and waited for spring to come so she could distill the orange blossoms into a fragrant water that lasted for hours on her skin. She plunged her hands with fervor into the special dough, rich with ghee butter and semolina, to make sweet *mafroukeh* dessert for the man of the house. He would joke with her, and she would ask him to play "the Carmen song" as she called it, and she would dream of the day when she would start bringing her daughter with her to the house and Ismail would suddenly appear before them, because Abdelkarim had sworn to her that there was no way he would not come back. He had to return the raincoat and pick up his wild azarole tree.

"Look. I put his name on it. Boil the water first, don't forget, before you water it."

They kept Ismail's secret between the two of them. After consulting Abdelkarim, Intisar decided, for Ismail's protection, to put off telling her husband that their son was still alive and was living somewhere nearby. Bilal Muhsin had gone back to roaming the city souks and the stairways of the American Quarter with a renewed appetite for talking. Every day he set out to narrate a new chapter in the saga of his heretofore unknown heroic deeds in the Bab al-Hadid rebellion, adding his martyred son's deeds into the mix, but he never could find anyone with the patience to listen to him.